Love Running Wild

AMY DENNIS

Love Running Wild

ISBN: 979-8-9891646-2-2

Title Credit: Kyle Bray
Editor: Lisa Thompson
Cover Design/Format: Alice Briggs @Kingdom Covers

Disclaimer:

This book is a work of fiction. All names, individuals, characters, businesses, places, and events in this book are either a product of the author's imagination or used fictitiously. Any resemblance to actual persons, living or dead, or actual events is purely coincidental.

The language is PG-13 and includes some swear words to stay true to the themes. This book deals with sensitive topics, including teenage drinking, drug use, domestic violence, sexual promiscuity, and abortion. As a Christian, I feel it is important to write Luca's story in a way that brings modern and real issues into the light, thus making them more readily available for discussion between parents and their children. These real-world situations need to be openly confronted, not hidden as though they don't exist. We don't want our next generations to be clueless, or worse, to be in danger when they eventually stumble upon situations such as these. These topics are realities that need to be bravely, openly, and non-judgmentally addressed by parents and young adults in our harsh world.

I wrote this book for anyone who feels unloved. If you are going through any of the situations in this fictional work, know that I understand how real and hurtful any of these matters can be. And I am praying that each and every one of you, my readers, will know that you are loved.

Dedication

As always, I would like to dedicate this book to my husband, Bill, who is my number one fan and encourager. Without his cheering me on and giving me constant support and input, I doubt any of my books would have been completed. I love you madly.

Second, I would like to dedicate this book to our sons and their wives: Payne (Jenny) and Joe (Cat).

To our nieces and nephew: Jordan, Marie, and Caleb. We love you.

And suddenly, I get to toss in an extra dedication. While writing this, our first grandson was born. Beau, you are only a week old, but you are precious and loved beyond the moon and stars.

To Janie, our first granddaughter, you are a gingersnap full of songs, laughter and sass. Nan and Papa can't wait until our next sleepover!

And finally, to you, my reader. You believed in me enough to spend your precious time and money on this book. You are helping my dreams become reality. My hope is that I am filling your world with hope and light. I am grateful to you beyond words. Thank you. Thank you. Thank you. Without you, my years of struggle were for nothing. I truly hope you enjoy the story of Luca.

Contents

Age Seven

OH NO. HERE she comes. I'm being so quiet, just like Mommy always wants. My dollies are being very quiet too. Mommy is screaming. Again. I stop brushing my dolly's hair and sit very, very still. I curl up into a tiny ball and rub my tummy. It always starts to hurt when Mommy yells. In the corner of my bright yellow bedroom, I listen. Is she coming? I don't know why Mommy's always mad.

She yells at me a lot. I don't like it. I feel so yucky inside. And scared. I hope she will stop it. I always try to be very good and very quiet, as quiet as a mouse. If I keep sitting really still and stay really, really quiet, then maybe she won't be mad anymore.

Uh-oh. My quiet isn't working. Her yelling is getting louder and stomp stomp stomp. She's coming down the hall. I quit being still and jump up fast. I want to run and hide, but she is right here in my room. She's too fast, holding my arm too tight and yanking me around. She grabs the sides of my face, squeezing so hard that her fingers make a fish mouth with my little lips and my teeth cut the inside of my cheeks. She screams ugly names at me.

Ouch! She yanks my face up to hers and stares into my eyes really mean. Our faces are right by each other. Our noses almost touch, and all I can smell is her yucky wine breath. She hates me! Tears fill my green eyes. I'm scared. *Why does Mommy hate me?* She won't let go of my face. She just keeps squeezing so hard. I can't move. *Please let go*, I think. *You are hurting me*!

She shrieks, "I wish I never had you! You should just run away! You are a mistake! Nobody loves you! Nobody wants you!"

I start to cry. Her stinky, wet drunk drops of spit are splashing onto my face, and I want to wipe them off. I cry harder. Mommy rolls her eyes in disgust, letting go of my face as she shoves me away from her in one quick push. I fall backwards onto my pile of dolls and toys, twisting my wrist when I land with a thud. I start crying even harder as I grab my wrist. "Ow!" I wail, in a lengthy cry.

"Oh. Just. Shut. Up!" She storms out of the room, slamming the door behind her.

I grab my favorite doll with my arm that's not hurt and cuddle her, rocking back and forth, back and forth, back and forth. Sometimes after Mommy acts mean to me, I suck my thumb. Even though I'm a big girl and I know I shouldn't, it makes me feel better.

I will hide in my room and suck my thumb, carefully because my wrist still hurts, until Daddy gets home from work. Then I will be safe from Mommy. Mommy never acts like this around Daddy. She hides her meanness from him and her wine too. *I'm sorry I'm not a good girl, Mommy. I will try harder. I just want you to love me.*

Age Thirteen

I AM SICK AND tired of Dad always grounding me. I'm honestly grounded all the time for doing nothing. The problem is that Mom still hates me. She makes up lies about me and tells Dad that I've done something wrong just so he will punish me. She plays mind games and bullies me. Plus, she tries to manipulate everything I do.

Well, news flash, Mom! You can't control me. I'm sneaking out tonight with some friends, so I'll be the one playing the games this time. Grounded or not, I am going to have fun. I have to get out of this house. If I don't, I might go crazy. I'm serious.

All of Mom's yelling, screaming, hair pulling, and hitting me is the worst. I can't make myself any more invisible or quiet than I already do, and I'm still not good enough or quiet enough for her to just leave me alone. I'm so excited for tonight. I'm nervous too. I hope I don't get caught trying to get out of the house.

I usually go to bed around nine thirty, and that's what time it is now. I've got to force myself to stay awake. My friends and I have a plan we've been working on for weeks. I think it's a pretty good one even though I've never snuck out before. Tonight, my act for Mom and Dad must be perfect. I will pretend to go to bed as usual, but I'm really going to be lying under my covers, waiting for them to fall asleep. Then, as soon as the coast is clear, I can boogie on out of here.

Our meetup is set for midnight. Several of the cool junior high kids, including me, have been invited to a huge party out in the cornfield between this town and the next. That's what we do for fun here in the Midwest. I can't wait! I've heard about these parties for a long time. Now, I'm finally going to one! My heart pounds. I have to act normal so Dad doesn't realize something's up. He's my more observant parent by far, and he hasn't been drinking tonight, so he's still wide awake.

I casually peek around the corner from the kitchen into our small living room to tell my parents I'm going to bed. "Goodnight," I holler at them both.

Dad looks up at me from the paper he's reading. "Goodnight." Mom is watching MTV and is probably drunk per her usual. Either that, or she just dislikes me so much these days that I'm no longer worth a reply. She doesn't look up from Madonna singing on the screen or acknowledge me. Whatever. I'm tired of her either screaming at me or acting like I don't exist. Rolling my eyes, I rush down the hall to the bathroom.

Examining my face carefully in the mirror, I check to make sure my makeup looks flawless. I touch up my curls with hairspray as quietly as I can, hoping the psst psst psst of the Aqua Net spraying doesn't give me away. Hairspray has never sounded so loud before. After rolling on a coat of clear, bubblegum-flavored lip gloss, I recap it and shove the tube into my front pocket. Adding a thick coat of purple mascara to my lashes, I stare at my reflection, smile, and wink. Dressed in my skintight Cindy Lauper T-shirt and denim cut-off daisy dukes, I look pretty hot. My dark hair shines, the long strands flowing effortlessly down my back. The violet mascara makes the green in my eyes pop.

While brushing my teeth, I try to recreate the regular sounds of washing my makeup off before bed, just in case Dad's listening. I'm not really washing my makeup off, of course. The running water, intentionally banging the cabinets open and shut, and scooting the soap dispenser loudly around on the counter are all just for effect.

I grab the bottle of NoDoz I bought earlier from my purse. Pulling the cottony wad out of the top, I shake two tablets into my palm. Gulping them down with warm, gross water from the bathroom faucet, I gag a little on the pills. These are supposed to keep a person awake for hours, and I'm about to find out if they work. I re-apply more lip gloss, smack my lips together twice, and shove the glass tube into my pocket again. I pee, then head to my room, sliding under the covers of my bed fully dressed. I'm careful to place my head on my pillow so that I don't mess up my hair. I lay on my back. Uptight, stiff, and unmoving, I wait.

I don't feel anything from the pills yet, and this is already taking forever. Minutes feel like hours. I wonder who will be at the party. I plan my escape route, going over in my mind exactly how I'm going to creep down the hall to get out of here. I nervously wonder if my friends will be outside or if they will ditch me since the girls giving me a ride are several years older than I am. I hope I won't be late. I twiddle my thumbs. I count to a thousand. I say the Pledge of Allegiance in my head. Twice. *Come on Mom and Dad, go to bed already*, I think.

The clock in the hall ticktocks, ticktocks along and finally chimes eleven. It's almost time! Mom and Dad have *got* to go to sleep soon. I have to be on time so my friends don't leave without me. Finally! The floor creaks; it's the worn spot in front of their bedroom door. Dad will be in bed and asleep within minutes. I'm antsy. I need to get going, but I don't want to move yet. I'm terrified of making any noise that would alert Dad and make him get back up to check the house. I wait a few more minutes. My heartbeat sounds as loud as a bass drum in my ears. Boom-boom! Boom-boom! Boom-boom!

Mom is probably still passed out downstairs. My heart's beating really fast now, more like a snare drum. Rat-a-tat! Rat-a-tat! Rat-a-tat! Rat-a-tat! I'm not sure if it's pounding is from the pills or the excitement. I picture myself somewhere out in the country, having fun and searching for love tonight, just like I do every time I get away from this place. That's what I do. I look for love. My mind drifts. Maybe my problem with finding love is that I have been going out with boys my age. I'm only thirteen, and thirteen-year-old boys don't care about my constant need or hunger for a serious relationship.

I am desperate for a real connection, dying for affection. All I dream about is being with someone who gives me true love. I really like kind words plus plenty of hugs, kisses, and lots of handholding. I want all the PDA. I yearn to be with someone who's not embarrassed to say, "Look at her! She's all mine," and then plant a big kiss right on my lips in front of everyone. But thirteen-year-old boys only want to play soccer and video games and look at boobs. The boys are *very i*nterested in my boobs, and *they* get a lot of attention. Boys at school take time to sweet talk me for a week or two until they can get me alone and grab a handful. I don't care, and I let them. I do care that a squeeze of the ole knockers is *all* they want. I care that they don't want *me.* Then they go bragging to their buddies that they got to feel me up, lots of times lying about other things that did not actually happen, making me sound easy. I found that out the hard way.

I'm not easy, but I have had sex. When I wanted to. On my terms. I'm not sure how normal that is at my age. It's not like girls talk about it, and even if they do, you never know if they're telling the truth about what did or didn't happen. You know, to save face or whatever. Guys get to brag about sex, and I have come to the conclusion that, a lot of times, they are lying about it too but for different reasons. Boys lie to try to look cool, which is so dumb. Girls can't say they did *anything* without everyone thinking they are a whore, so they lie and say *nothing* happened.

I'm. Over. The. Teenage. Boys. I may only be thirteen, but I feel like I'm twenty. I've already lived through a lot, and I'm really trying to find my person. I need a man—not a child—who will understand the depths of my soul. I have an internal drive to find him. I'm looking all the time, everywhere I go. I feel like I'm starving to death. For love, not for food. That might sound crazy at my age, but I've lived with hate for thirteen years. That's my whole life! I'm exhausted. Not physically but emotionally. I do have a lot to offer the right guy. After all, there is love running wild in my soul.

My mind drifts back to the boys. They all like me when they meet me because I can be lots of fun and like I said, I have huge boobs. But then, the next thing you know, they're saying I'm too clingy. I just think they aren't mature enough to give me what I need emotionally. So, I've decided to start looking for a real man, someone older. And I'm gonna have a great time looking for him too. I *will* find the right man to love me.

Laying here, waiting for the clock to strike midnight, I'm starting to feel like Cinderella. Well, if Cinderella was a slut. Ha. Ha. Maybe my dream of finding my prince will come true tonight. It's almost time to find out! There's been no movement in the hall for at least fifteen minutes, so I think it's probably safe now. Slowly sitting up, I wait a beat. Then, getting out of my bed, a spring squeaks. I'm instantly still. I feel like I'm the bunny on one of those nature shows, hopping happily along, but then, all of a sudden, sensing danger, it sits totally still, only its nostrils flaring wildly. I pause. Listen. No noise. I proceed with caution.

I slip my purse over my shoulder. I have no idea why I need my purse in the middle of the night, but better safe than sorry, right? I tiptoe to my bedroom door and slowly turn the brass knob opening it. So far, so good. I've barely made a sound. Holding my breath, I step out cautiously. I silently exhale while quickly and quietly pulling the wooden door closed. My palms are getting sweaty. My eyes adjust to the inky darkness as silence surrounds me.

Starting to walk down the now darkened hall, I glance into the living room. Mom is still right where she was before, in front of the tv. She's snoring, passed out cold. I've already made it to the front door. I still need to put on my shoes and steady myself with a hand against the wall, sliding my feet around in the dark, one at a time, until I slip into each white Ked. I'm almost out of the house!

I inhale through my nose and exhale silently through my mouth to slow my heart and steady my hands. I reach for the front doorknob and twist. My hands are still a little shaky, but the door clicks open easily. I step over the threshold onto the porch, and I'm outside. Pulling the door shut behind me, I start to briskly jog away from the dark house. A little further down the road, I stop jogging and walk. I don't want to be all sweaty and gross when I get to the party.

My hands tremble just a bit as the rest of my adrenaline rush wears off. I fish around in my denim purse for the pack of Capri cigarettes I have stashed inside. After I pull out the semi-smashed pack, I scrounge around for my lighter. Finding it, I tap a cig out of my half-smoked pack and light up with a flick of my Bic. Taking the first smooth drag, I inhale deeply, then puff smoke from my mouth and nose. I feel satisfied. Content. This sneaking-out stuff is great. Being out and about while most of the world sleeps is exhilarating. Everything looks and even smells different at night. I feel grown-up, like there's an entire unexplored world right at my fingertips.

My girlfriend's bright yellow Chevy Impala is parked and waiting at the end of the street, just where she said it would be. The headlights are off, but the car is still running. The engine purrs like a jungle cat. As I approach, we mutter quick hellos, and then I climb clumsily into the back where my friends are already piled on the pleather bench seat. I end up splayed crookedly across everyone's laps, our legs all tangled up. Jenny, who owns this badass car, slams the door shut, flips the headlights on, and cranks the radio up. We start cruising.

For the night, we've all brought booze. It's so easy for us girls to get it. No liquor store in the 1980s cards cute girls even though there is no way we look twenty- one. Most of us still have braces. A few of us have connections to get pot, which is also pretty easy to score if you're female. So we have crinkled up baggies of seedy ditch weed too. We pass around a couple of joints my friend Joey rolled for me and do shots, taking swigs of vodka straight from the bottle on the drive. In the hour it takes us to find the cornfield, the car has become hazy with smoke even though the windows are rolled halfway down.

None of us is totally sober when we arrive, but we aren't shit-faced either. We're all just relaxed and ready for more of a good time. The gravel road is dark and haphazardly lined with cars parked on either side. A river rushes by somewhere in the distance, and fireflies intermittently glow, floating on the summer breeze. As we park, I poke my head out of the now completely rolled-down window of the car. My eyes slowly adjust to our rural surroundings.

Country music from someone's boombox drifts through the darkness. The smell of beer and cigarette smoke mix together with the aroma of manure from the nearby farms and the crisp night air. It smells wild, like the promise of adventure. The half-moon and a few bright stars above give off hints of light, but the night remains inky black. Corn stalks stand at attention in shadowy rows like soldiers on guard. The random flicker of orange-red flames from lighters firing up a joint or occasional long, blinding yellow beams from incoming headlights illuminate our dusty gathering as new groups of teens arrive. These are the only things that occasionally pierce the darkness that envelops us but is alive with activity.

Buzzed, I already feel more peace here than I ever do at home. *This is gonna be fun,* I. Since my head and shoulders are already sticking out of the open car window, I suddenly decide to climb out of the window instead of opening the door. I do a dismount Dukes of Hazzard–style, and as I'm clawing my way outside, as lady-like as possible, my gaze is drawn to a guy I don't recognize standing across the road. He's facing our car, smoking and watching me inquisitively. In the moonlight, I can't really see his face, but I'm pretty sure he's cute. Really cute. I squint and stare to get a better look. *Is he my long- lost prince*? I wonder. Curious, I decide to find out.

Not waiting for my friends, I finish my less than graceful descent from the car window, scraping my shin as it slides through the opening. Almost falling face first, I catch myself roughly, landing on my palms before my feet (thankfully) hit the ground. I quickly adjust myself and brush the newly imbedded gravel and dirt from my hands, then take off across the road toward the mystery man.

The cute guy has his back to me now and is standing talking casually with a small circle of people who appear several years older than I am. Having had enough vodka to feel brave, I walk right up behind the handsome stranger and tap him solidly, twice on the shoulder. *What am I doing*? I think as I continue tapping him. When he turns around, I instantly see that he's waaay ho tter than I had originally thought. My heart flutters, and a knot forms like a ball in my stomach. An undeniable spark of something shoots between us as our eyes meet. In a split second, I grab him and kiss him on the lips, all in one unstoppable, electric moment. He does not argue or push me away. Surprisingly, he grabs my waist firmly, pulls me into him, and keeps right on kissing me. French kisses. *Yesss*!

After several deliciously long seconds, he steps back, giving me an inquisitive look and lopsided smile. I smile back, and then our lips are connecting again. *This is going to be awesome*, I think, as his warm, soft lips press against mine. His kisses taste like beer, and he smells like Old Spice. Delicious! "Get a room!" some guy grumbles as he turns and walks away. A couple of the girls in the group start whispering to each other, and a couple of the other people just wander off. I couldn't care less about the others standing there. We just keep kissing and then take a breather, staring at each other with goofy smiles. I pull back a little, making eye contact again. "Hi," I say.

"Hey," he says back as our lips come together in tiny, hungry kisses.

He grabs my hand and stops kissing my mouth long enough to brush his lips, in small gentle bites, against the base of my neck and all the way up until they find my ear. He nibbles it and whispers, "Let's go find somewhere more private." Then he pulls me toward the field. On the way to our more secluded spot, he swipes a couple of ice-cold bottles of beer out of a banged-up red-and-white Igloo cooler that sits opened, unattended on the tailgate of some stranger's Ford. I have a bottle opener on my key ring. Fishing around in my purse, I find it and quickly pry the tops off the slick, amber bottles. I take a quick gulp of mine as I hand my newfound friend his own refreshing brewski.

Wandering deep into a field, we frantically kiss and grope each other in between ice cold swigs of Bud. Our hands are flying all over each other's bodies in a frenzy of youth and passion as we disappear into the privacy of our own darkened row of corn. I accidentally slosh some of my frigid beer down his back, but he doesn't seem to notice.

I have no idea where my friends are, and honestly, I don't care. This guy is so hot! And he's a really great kisser. Our bodies fit together as perfectly as they can through our clothing, the sparks between us growing more intense with each moment. We can't keep our hands or our mouths off each other, and before I know it, we are half-naked in the dirt and husks. Well, he is naked. I still have my shirt on, because you know, people are around. Someone could wander over and see me. That's not happening, so I intend to stay mostly clothed.

His body in the moonlight is lean and … hard. As good as he looked in his Wranglers and Ariat boots, he looks better without them. Bending over, he arranges our crumpled clothing into a small pile and eases me down onto the impromptu bed, continuing what we started. I am not a virgin, but I am still nervous to have sex with him because he is really, really cute. I want this night to end well so that maybe we can eventually fall in love. You know, in the future. *Sex can end in love, can't it?* I ask myself. A picture of life with him flashes in my mind like a movie. Feeling overwhelmed with good emotions, I almost tear up. I imagine that the excitement I'm feeling right now is how true love must start.

I lay on my back, the ground softened by our clothing under me, staring up at the night sky. He is laying on his side next to me, stretched out so that his toned stomach brushes my side. He rests his head on his hand and stares down at me, not speaking. I run my fingers over his strong, steady arm. His skin is smooth and warm. He leans into me, our bodies touching, legs entwined, as he whispers sweet things in my ear. The gentle stroking motions as he runs his fingertips over my body calm me, excite me, and give me goosebumps all at the same time. I want more. I need more. We gently kiss. The kisses become more frantic, and before I know it, we have just had what I judge to be *way* above average sex. We lay there, covered in sweat and dirt.

We both chug the rest of our now warm beer as we snuggle together silently in the semi- privacy of a million corn husks. Stars twinkling overhead and the sound of crickets chirping make time seem to stand still. For at least a couple of hours, our hearts seem to be beating in unison. My soul feels hopeful. So far, tonight has been amazing. My buzz from the weed and booze wore off hours ago, but I've got a different kind of buzz going on now. It's pure delight. And obviously, more than a little bit of lust. The once inky sky is turning a much lighter gray-orange, signaling that sunrise is near.

I slowly untangle my body from his. Getting up, I brush off as much dirt as I can from my sweat-tinged body while I pull on my underwear and shorts. I slip my tennis shoes back on and wander several rows away to squat and pee, being careful to spread my feet far enough apart so that I don't get them wet. When I find my way back to where we have just been lying together minutes before, I can't seem to find him. My lover is gone. Just like that. *What? Am I misunderstanding something?* Or maybe I'm lost, but I *know* I'm in the right spot. The impressions our bodies made together are still here in the dirt, along with our empty beer bottles.

My heart sinks a little, and now I really do feel like Cinderella. My prince has disappeared into the night. Poof! I should have known better. All the older folks in town are always saying nothing good happens after midnight. Maybe I should have listened to them. Too late now. I wander, searching methodically up and down a few of the rows, sometimes cutting between them, working my way back toward the road. At first, I yell out hopefully, thinking he will reappear. When he doesn't show, I start begging and pleading for him to please, please, come out of wherever it is he has gone. I'm not proud of the begging, but I'm hoping maybe he's just trying to be funny and is hiding. As I call out with no response, my hope quickly fades. A motor starts up and drives away in the not-too-far-off distance. Is it him? I don't know. Hell, I don't even know if he has a car.

I thought maybe this magical night would turn into the love I was looking for, but now I realize it was just another one-night stand. Worse than that, the whole time we were together, I never even asked his name. *How* could I never ask him his *name*? I mean, how does that happen? I know it sounds absurd, but I'll tell you how. We were just so busy kissing, drinking beer, and making awkward googly eyes at each other. Then we clicked and felt so comfortable together that it felt like we had been friends forever, like I already knew him. Next thing you know, we just started screwing, and the night seemed to be over in the blink of an eye. We barely even *talked* at all. How stupid!

My dream of finding love tonight has turned into a pumpkin, or maybe, in this case, an ear of corn. The moment was so fun, but now I'm left with the distinct feeling that again, I mean nothing to anyone. I am alone and disposable. At least whoever he was, he was nice to me for the night. *Just keep looking for love. It has to be out there*, I tell my heartbroken self, as I start the long, solitary walk home. As I walk, I also remind myself that I didn't really know him at all. And he was so cute that I was overwhelmed in the moment and didn't even think to make him wear a condom. *That was dumb. I hope he didn't give me chlamydia.* The thought shoots through my brain before I even know it. The fun of the night has definitely worn off. Bummer.

Age Sixteen

IT'S ALMOST CHRISTMAS! The lights and music always make it feel as if magic is alive in the air. Magic and hope. That's why this season is my favorite time of year. I could stare at Christmas lights and listen to holiday classics year-round. They both make me feel lighter inside, like just about anything is possible. During this festive season, every year feels like *this* just might be the year. The year that I finally find love.

As much as I adore the festivities, there are also a couple of things I never look forward to. First, while I feel hopeful, I also always feel extra alone during the holidays. The movies, music, and decorations keep me distracted from that fact, but when I see happy families and large groups of friends out enjoying each other's company, I feel more isolation and solitude than normal. I mean, I have Dad, but he's always at work trying to get enough sales to receive the big Christmas bonus his company dangles just beyond his reach each year. I don't even see him for days on end. When I do happen to run into him, he's so stressed by the time he gets home that he just shuffles silently to his chair in the living room where he reads the newspaper and guzzles cheap bourbon. There he remains sullen in his silent solitude until he's ready for bed. I'm usually asleep by then, but he does the same thing almost every night.

The other thing is that Mom drinks even more than usual this time of year too. Her drunkenness makes her extra hateful and depressed from the beginning of November to well after the New Year. She says drinking gives her "Christmas cheer." I say, she is full of bah humbug. There's nothing cheerful about her constant intoxication and anger. I try my best to steer clear of her. I sneak out all the time now. Mom and Dad have no idea, or if they do, they don't care enough to try to stop me. My goal is to never be at home except to sleep. I cannot mentally take the daily rants and drama anymore. I really need to find my man because I'm just positive that he's going to be my ticket out of all this. He and I will be able to start a whole new life together and live happily ever after. Far, far away from here.

I keep going on date after date. Some (ok, many) turn into one -night stands, but no one can say I'm not giving my dream my full attention. I'm not going to give up, but I am becoming more and more anxious about finding love. I need to permanently get away from the mental hell that I live in with my parents. Every second around them is awful. Mom just cannot say anything nice to me, period. With Dad, it's hit or miss, depending on if he's drunk or sober.

How many times do I need to hear that I am not wanted and unloved? How many times do I have to be hit and smacked and grabbed? I'm pretty sure I'd really enjoy living somewhere I don't get yanked around by my hair. How often do I have to hear sober morning apologies from Dad that I just start to believe when he gets shit-faced and hits me again? When do I get to live where Mom isn't screaming names at me as she drunkenly attacks me, clawing my face? I've gotten their message loud and clear. I am alone and unwanted. For those that doubt its existence, mental torment is an actual thing. I live it. No one is looking out for me and no one has my back. This house is only a building. Sure, it's a shelter from outside storms, but sometimes the storms in here are much worse. This building is not a true home. Home is supposed to be a safety net for me to fall into when the world gets tough. This definitely isn't that.

That's why I'm working really hard, always trying to meet up with new guys, and saving money to get away. Well, now that I've brought up the whole working and money thing, that leads me to item number three that I despise during the holidays: present buying. Right now, I'm dating a guy named Ryan who is very nice to me. He's just not really what I'm looking for long-term, I'm sure of that much. I've sort of been debating breaking up with him. He's just a space filler for when I'm lonely or bored. That sounds bitchy, but it's true, and I'm being honest here. Ryan is a genuinely kind person. And he has a wonderful, safe home where I can hang out pretty much whenever I need to. I feel guilty for wanting to break up with him. I feel guilty for not wanting to buy him a present. I mean, not that I don't really want to, but the thought of what to buy, how much to spend, when to give it to him, and all that stuff stresses me the hell out.

I also feel guilty for not going ahead and breaking up with him because I know I'm wasting his time in the long run and he hasn't done anything wrong. I'm keeping him around for his kindness, and I don't think that's very nice of me. It just feels so good knowing that at least someone in the world cares about me. That is hard to let go of. Is that bad? I don't know. Sometimes I feel like it is, but on my quest for true love, I just have to do what I have to do. I guess I'm working up the nerve to break it off before Christmas. That means I definitely won't have to buy a present for him. The whole present buying thing makes me feel very pressured and uneasy. Mom says I never get gift giving right even when I really try. So I would rather just break up with him to avoid all of this internal pressure on myself. Plus, I really, really, really need to save every penny. Saved pennies equal my getting my new life sooner rather than later.

Mom has always told me that I'm some kind of huge failure. I guess her attitude has finally rubbed all the way off on Dad because now he tells me I'm a disappointment almost as often as she does. Mom still screams all kinds of crap at me anytime she has the chance. And I still don't understand how or why she hates me this much. I'm going to school and working. And gol dang, I'm only sixteen. I'm not sure how that makes me a failure or a loser but whatever. Mom's verbal and physical attacks are draining and humiliating. She grabs me and hits me and pushes me and smacks me, all while calling me every name in the book. The fact that Dad joins in now when he's drunk, which is becoming almost daily, is even worse. I used to think he was on my side. Not anymore. Now, I'm more alone than ever.

I've been feeling extra tense and down this year, so I decided to put the Christmas tree up by myself last week when Mom and Dad were both gone. I'm very happy with my spontaneous decision. Now, when life looks dark and bleak, I can just plug in those lights, and bam!—a tiny flicker of Christmas hope ignites inside me. Sitting here now in the tree's warm, cozy, multi-colored glow helps cheer me up in some tiny, festive way. The lights are twinkly and look almost alive with Christmas spirit, and I adore the piney smell too. I also love looking at all the random ornaments I've collected over the years. Hanging each one on the tree makes me happy. A fragile memory of something good. As I sit here zoned out, gazing at the tall, green fir, I decide that all I'm missing is a drink.

I know where Mom hides her stash of wine, so I grab a bottle, unscrew the cap, and help myself. Mom is at church for a tent revival meeting. Good. That thing will last hours and hours, which means I get to relax and enjoy being cozy here on the couch, undisturbed and peaceful in my snuggly blanket with a bottle of sweet red and my cat, ironically named Cat, curled in my lap. *Miracle on 34th Street* is just starting on TV. Perfect timing. It's my very favorite Christmas movie. By the time Mom gets back and Cad gets home from work, I will be a much happier, drunk sixteen- year- old. Even if Mom screams ugly names at me, which she probably will, nothing she says will hurt my feelings. I won't allow it. I will have a wonderfully numb heart and mind. She will *not* steal my Christmas spirit. Fa la la la la.

Well, my movie has ended. I must have dozed off from the wine. The TV's still on, but it's just playing that black-and-white fuzzy static noise. Stretching, I rub my eyes. I drank the entire original bottle of wine I took from Mom's stash, plus half of another one. It went down easy. Mom may or may not notice that I took it, but I mean, what's she gonna do? Report to Dad that I stole the wine she hides from him? Please. I don't think so. Wine and Christmas music go wonderfully together anyway, like jingle goes with bells, like Rudolf goes with red-nosed reindeer, like Frosty goes with snowman.

I stretch out again and the cat stretches too. I gently pat him as we both get up from the couch. I've decided that what I would enjoy now are some Christmas tunes. I snap the TV off and shuffle over to the record player. Digging through the pile of records that Dad keeps stored in an old red plastic Coca-Cola crate, I grab a retro album whose faded cover has a cartoonish drawing of Rudolph. I carefully slip the record out of its paper sleeve and, holding it by its edges, place it gently on the player. I bet this thing is from the 1940s or 50s. It has all the original Christmas classics by the old singers like Bing Crosby and Andy Williams. I gently lift the arm on the record player and the album spins. When the needle connects, the room comes alive with sound. There's nothing like the crackly, static pops of music on vinyl. Something about it combined with the vintage music makes life seem a little more solid. Like everything will somehow turn out all right. Every cell in my body absorbs the music on these records for hours.

Well, Mom is still not home from church, and Dad still isn't home from work (or most likely, the bar). I am getting lonely and restless. I call Ryan to see what he's up to. As we talk on the phone, I wander around the house as far as the stretched-out cord will let me, pulling it out from the wall where the phone is attached and twisting it, twirling, and untwisting it from around my body as we talk. He says he's not doing anything and invites me over. I twist and twirl with the phone cord some more as I think of what answer to give him. *Should I break up with him right now,* I ask myself, *or should I go over and hang out because I'm bored? Hmm.* Twisting my dark hair around my finger, I think it over for a minute.

I twirl some more in my socked feet, sliding on the tiled floor to the sounds of Brenda Lee's "Rockin' Around the Christmas Tree," giving an extra big spin and shimmy as the song ends. I bow for my invisible audience and feel so happy and carefree in the moment that I almost get the nerve to break up with him. Almost. Instead, in a split-second decision, I decide that I might as well go hang at his house. Telling him I'll be over, I hang up. I throw on my favorite hoodie and grab the keys to the old banged-up Plymouth Scamp Dad got me by trading some work with a buddy.

I step outside into the crisp winter night and pull the hood over my head with a shiver. The sting of the freezing air burns my face, but the wine keeps the rest of my body warm. The neighbors' Christmas lights look blurry in the distance. I rub my eyes with my fists and blink a bunch to clear them. Nope. Still blurry. I don't think I'm super drunk or anything, but I decide to drive extra carefully. Just in case. Maybe I am still just a bit tipsy, but it's been hours since my last drink. I'm sure it'll be fine. It's not that far of a drive to Ryan's, and I'll be cautious. *Go slow and be extra careful,* I tell myself as I hop in the Scamp, buckle the lap belt, stick the key in the ignition, and start the car. She roars to life. Turning the heater on full blast, adjusting the vents, and dialing the radio to the FM station that plays Christmas carols this time of year, I back slowly out of the drive, and I'm on my way.

The back roads to Ryans' house are all gravel. They are traffic-free, making the drive enjoyable. I'm glad to be out and about. The Christmas tunes I have blaring from the radio are keeping me in my festive mood. I cruise along, drumming my fingers on the steering wheel, singing at the top of my lungs. "*Fiiive goldeeen riiings*!" Every house I pass (which isn't many out here in the boonies) has holiday decorations up, which makes me feel even more festive. My eyes are drawn this way, then that way, taking in the displays as I journey along the country wonderland.

Relaxed by the music and the open road, I lose track of how fast I'm going. I've also forgotten about the wine I knocked back earlier. The road is curvy and dark with days' old packed snow, making it invisibly slick in spots. A gazillion white snow flurries flutter down and fly past my windshield. Coming faster and faster, illuminated by my headlights, they create a dizzying effect. The image reminds me of The Millenium Falcon whizzing through a galaxy in *Star Wars*.

The flakes and the darkness simultaneously start to cover the beams of my headlights, making it difficult to see. I turn on the wipers to clear my view through the glass, but the snow freezing onto the windshield just streaks into one big icy smear. Passing a house with one of those huge, inflatable snow globes in the front yard, I glance over at it, the light and motion drawing my eyes from the road. Along with the snow globe are displays of red-and-white candy canes that look real enough to eat. An inflatable, cheerful Santa waves to passersby in his sleigh with a big velvet sack of toys thrown over one shoulder. Animated elves climb ladders. Life-size stacks of illuminated presents sparkle, and large twinkling snowflakes dangle effortlessly from the trees. It looks like Hobby Lobby threw up. It is over-the-top tacky, and I love every bit of it! There's even a manger scene. *Oh look! There's baby… Jesus!* My rear tires slip and slide for a few seconds, reminding me to slow down as my heart skips a beat.

I hit the brakes as I glance at the speedometer. *Seventy miles per hour? Crap, that's too fast.* I immediately start to let off the brakes as hitting them is making the car slide more. Too late. The car is spinning in wild circles. I try to hold the sliding car onto the road with all my strength focused on controlling the steering wheel, but it's not working. I'm on a sheet of ice and overcorrecting. I can't see anything. The car flies, sailing and swirling through a blinding dark sea of nothingness. *Wham*! Impact.

My face slams hard onto the steering wheel, and my head snaps back up as the car starts to spin the other way. Now, I'm pressing as hard as I can on the brakes and holding onto the steering wheel with a death grip. The car finally glides to a stop. *Hoooly snowballs*! My heart feels like it's about to pound out of my chest. Warmth that I assume is blood is trickling out of my nose. Reaching up to check it, I wince. The bridge is all lumpy. I know without looking that it's broken. I pinch it painfully hard with my left hand to help stop the bleeding as I open the glove box with my right. I rustle around in the darkness, trying to find something I can use as a tissue. I find what I think is an old napkin and press it to my nose. I sit and gather myself for a few moments, taking deep breaths through my mouth since I'm clamping my nose to staunch the flow of blood oozing from it.

Once I get my nosebleed under control, I slowly check each arm and leg by moving them to see if everything still works. Arms-check. Legs-check. I twist my head from side to side, up and down. Head and neck, good. Nothing but my nose hurts. Now, I wonder what I hit. I try to get out of the driver's door but it's jammed shut. Scooting and scooching clumsily to the passenger side, I open that door with a few hard shoves and climb out of the car. Pulling my hood down tight around my head, and still occasionally wiping blood from my nose, I look right and left. I see dark brown, swirled skid marks in the gravel and snow where I spun. *Wait! What is that? I think I see something poking out of the snow. Is it an antler? Is it a…a…*reindeer? I ask myself in shock and awe. *Did I hit an actual reindeer?* I rub my eyes. *Oh, no, dumbass. That's the wine talking.* What looked like an antler for a second is actually the splintered wooden post of a mailbox that I have plowed into. Not a reindeer antler. *Good grief. I'm obviously not sober. You should not be driving,* I tell myself just a smidge too late. Dad is going to be really pissed off when he finds out about this. I feel very lucky that I didn't really hurt myself or anyone else. I send a quick mental *thank you* up to God.

Looking around, I realize that I am almost to Ryan's house and that it's freezing out. I climb back into the car through the passenger side to see if the car is drivable. The Scamp's engine is still running. That's a good sign. I shift the car into reverse, tapping the gas. The tires only spin with a whirring sound for a couple of minutes, but then, just as

I'm giving up hope, I finally grab some traction and slowly get back onto the road. I stop and buckle up, dabbing at my nose, which has now stopped bleeding. I turn the car around and head home as inflatable Santa waves bye. Santa, Rudolph, and the Baby Jesus are the only witnesses to this little event.

I'm not in the mood to see Ryan now at all. Knowing that I wrecked the car dad worked hard to get me bums me out. What a loser. Plus, now I'm nervous. I can't tell in the darkness what damage I have done, but the car is making weird noises, so I know I did something. Mom is already always mad. And I think this will set Dad off. We don't have money to fix whatever it is that I have done to the car, plus, even though he seems to like me less and less each year, I don't want to disappoint Dad more than I already have. It was stupid to drive after drinking all that wine. I won't tell him the drinking part, of course. I will blame it on the ice.

I drive home in silence, focusing on my speed and the road, thankful that I only hit a mailbox. No more drinking and driving is my lesson of the night. I arrive home and pull into our drive. Dad and Mom still aren't home. I go to bed after calling Ryan to let him know I'm not coming over. When the sun comes up tomorrow, the damage on the car will have to be looked at, and then I will have to tell Dad. I'm not looking forward to it. I will definitely be grounded. Again. I can picture Dad in the morning, looking at me with his sad, watery, hungover eyes, and telling me, "You're such a disappointment," as he tries to hide the fact that he now sneaks whiskey into his coffee first thing every day. Getting grounded for wrecking the car means that my hunt for true love will be on hold for a few weeks … again.

Age Seventeen

WELL, I CAME home from school today as Mom was backing out of our driveway in the truck. From what I could see, the truck was loaded down with what looked like most of her worldly possessions, but I don't know what set her off to leave or where she went. She didn't stop. She didn't even slow down to wave goodbye. She definitely saw me standing there because, hell, she had to swerve really quick to not run me over. Our eyes locked for the briefest second. Then she looked away. I feel something inside myself about it. Maybe it's a little twinge of sadness and shock that she left, but mostly, I just feel relieved. And I feel a little bit bad that I don't feel worse about the whole thing. I wonder if Dad will be upset when he finds out that she's gone. At least she won't be around to scream at me anymore. I guess I'll just see how it goes with Dad when he gets home. I am 100 percent sure that Mom's never coming back. I could tell by the look on her face. It's like we are already dead to her. Her eyes were glazed over and almost dead as she took that one quick glance my way. Well, good riddance then, I guess.

Age Seventeen and a Half

SINCE MOM LEFT, life has gone way down the tubes, and I, for one, cannot believe I'm saying that, considering how bad it was back then. Right before Mom left, I had started going back to church, I had yet another new boyfriend, and I was doing ok in school. All of that has gone to absolute shit. Now, Dad's a hard-core drunk. With Mom gone, he has no reason to hide his drinking anymore and no one to nag him to stop. The more he drinks, the worse he acts. Now he's seeing some skanky girl, and I don't like her. At. All. Her name is Janice. "Jan" for short.

While they're out drinking and doing Lord knows what, I do everything at home. All the laundry, cooking, cleaning, even grocery shopping is up to me. It sucks. All the chores at home take hours from my schoolwork, so I started flunking. My social life went to hell. My fairly normal boyfriend of a couple of months dumped me because I was too busy to ever hang out. Also, he realized my family was a complete trainwreck the first time he tried to hang out at my house and Dad met him, drunk on the porch with his wood-whittling knife and a carving of a tiny man. I guess Dad was yelling something like, "This could be you, son!" as he carved. Dad thought it was really funny. My boyfriend didn't find it so amusing. Who can blame him? I was pissed at Dad when I found out what he did, but I'm not that upset about this *particular* boyfriend being gone. All he ever wanted to do was snuggle while he watched some guy named Payne play golf on TV, and I was bored out of my mind the entire time. I barely had time to be with him anyway because once I get all the house stuff taken care of, which is basically an hour before I go to bed, I just want to sit down, exhausted from the day.

I stopped going to school a few weeks ago. I was flunking math from skipping class too much. I was skipping class because I knew I'd get sent to the office for not getting my homework done. I couldn't get all the homework done because of all the stuff I now have to take care of at home since Mom's gone. It's a vicious cycle. I'm just trying to hustle to survive. I already got a full-time job at the local Pump and Squirt gas station, and I also already went and took my GED test. That's the certificate you get that counts as a high school diploma. I signed up to take it and when I went that Saturday, I passed with flying colors! Go me. I had to take and pass that test before I could apply to college. That way, I can leave as soon as fall comes around. August is already only a few short months away.

I have everything planned out, and I know Dad has some money hidden away to help pay for classes. My budget will be tight, but Dad has promised for years that he will at least help pay for some college expenses, and I'm holding him to his word. Soon, I'll be out of his hair, and no one on campus will know this person I am right now. I'm going to totally re-invent myself. I'm excited about that part.

I'm sure Dad will be happy to have me gone. He's still being a jerk to me; plus, Jan is over at the house all the time. She basically lives here. Blah. I have to get out of here. So, per my plan, I'm applying to colleges every minute that I'm not working. On one hand, I have no idea what I'm doing and I sometimes feel like a drop-out loser. On the other hand, I'm excited about new possibilities. I still haven't found love. And finding it will still always be my main goal. I'm excited to be around an entirely new group of people. That will be good. I also think I need a fresh bunch of dudes to choose from. Now *that* has real possibilities. I'm going to get a fresh start. Watch out, college campus! Here I come. You won't be able to handle me.

Age Eighteen: Week One – College

I'M HERE! COLLEGE feels like a totally new life, and everything about it seems somehow better. I'm almost six hours away from my hometown and living in a dorm with a roommate that I hadn't met until yesterday. I've never had a roommate before but she's cool. We're getting all settled in. She and I bought a cool wooden bed frame made out of two by fours from some guys down the hall, and they helped us put it up so my sleeping area is up high like a loft bed on top of the wood frame. That gives us more living space underneath. The area is very small, so we will take any extra room we can get. I've already hung up a disco ball and strings of multicolored lights underneath the loft bed to keep the dorm from feeling so drab.

My roomie's bed is like a normal bedroom set up with her twin mattress resting on the campus provided cheap metal frame. I love being up in my little loft area with a bird's eye view of the room. It feels fun and different. It's like a half bunk bed, half tree house. It's way cool. The other students on our floor are slightly jealous that we lucked out and bought the bed before anyone else. It does give off awesome vibes. We definitely have the best room set up.

I've met tons of people already, and I've checked out some of the bars. It's pretty chill here, and I'm feeling good. The roomie and I decided to have a party in our dorm room this weekend. We've already bought a huge trash can to make the jungle juice in. We're trying to get other people on our floor to join in so we can wander from room to room, sort of like a bar crawl. We'll have to see how that goes. I'll update you later.

Update. Holy. Shit. The party was awesome! We met so many people! There were about ten different sets of roommates and suitemates that decided to join our party plan. Word got around, and I swear, half of the campus showed up. One room had a keg. We had jungle juice. Only one room didn't have booze because they were scared of getting busted, you know, minors in possession and all of that legal stuff. But it didn't matter at all that they didn't have any alcohol. We all just carried our Solo cups with us and kept going back for refills.

Plus, another room had weed, acid, shrooms, and who knows what else. I'm not really a fan of drugs, but as you'd expect, lots of the college kids here seem to be. I couldn't really care less. There was a gambling room for people throwing dice. I kissed the dice for good luck, for the hot guys only, of course. In another room, a big group was playing strip poker.

When I got to those people, I don't know why I joined in when they asked me to since I have no idea how to play, but I did. The guys and girls promised they'd explain the rules to me. To give them credit, they did try to teach me the basics; however, between the booze, music, and my lack of focus, I was down to my bra and panties in about five minutes. That's when I quit. I was definitely the loser. In fact, I was the only person in their underwear, and I was not about to get buck naked. I got redressed in a flash and moseyed my way over to the next room.

They had a Ouija board in there. Those kids were all sitting around in a circle, trying to get the thing to work. I didn't want anything to do with that devil stuff, so I left immediately. The last thing I need is some demons floating around in my life. (I'm not sure if they float exactly, but you know what I'm saying. Nope. Nope. Nope.) We all had our doors propped open so people could wander in and out as they wanted. Some girl had a huge green pet lizard on a little reptile leash and was letting everyone hold it. I think it was an iguana. That was pretty cool.

As you would expect, people were making out everywhere and dancing in the halls. There were all types of different music blaring from the different rooms. Wisps of pop, country, rap, and heavy metal smashed invisibly in the air together in the hallway until some loser poked his head out of his room and said he was going to narc us out to the RA and the cops if we didn't quiet down. So we quieted down. Well, a little. We all closed our doors, and suddenly, the one large party became several smaller, more intimate parties with whoever happened to be in whatever room they landed in.

I actually ended up back in my room dancing and pounding more jungle juice with some hot upper classman and other random coeds. Needless to say, our room had it going on. Everyone wanted our jungle juice. Somehow, I and one of the upperclassmen ended up naked, elevated above the party in my loft bed while the party raged on below. The lights were dimmed, the disco ball shimmered, and dance music was blasting so no one even knew we were up there. Well, until some other drunk couple tried to climb the ladder to use my bed, unaware that it was already occupied. As soon as the girl's head popped over the mattress edge, I yelled at them both, not too kindly, to "GTFO!" They were as surprised as we were. And GTFO they did. All in all, it was a huge success. College isn't half bad. I do have a splitting headache this morning though. I hope water, ibuprofen, and some saltines help.

Week Two – College

"WHO IS YOUR sister!? I am she! Who are your sisters!? The Zeta Bs!"

I can't believe that I'm here! I did it! I'm actually rushing sororities. The good ones. Talk about being the opposite of my life at home. I love all of this. These girls might end up being my "sisters." They are smart, beautiful, classy, rich, successful, and so far, it seems like they know how to have fun. I'm trying to dress more conservatively (less slutty) and just follow them around, mimicking them like all the girls rushing seem to do. The copycat thing is not really optional. I'm learning that just by observing the masses.

They all like to do things together and do them exactly the same way. They wear the same clothes. They do their hair the same way. They eat the same foods. And they like only a certain frat house so they like all the same guys. It's interesting and a little Stepford Wife-ish. But this is Greek life, and I'm hoping they will accept me. The Greek life still seems like the best option for me. This process is making me feel like maybe I'm not as bad as Mom and Dad always said. These girls seem to only notice the good qualities in me, but I'm a pledge, so I know they are truly judging me, like every single thing I say and do. It's just on the down low, quietly. And with a smile. Like the ladies do to people in the South. Whatever. At least they aren't telling me all of my faults to my face. It's a nice change from life at home.

I have high hopes that through them, I will change my life for the better and meet my perfect man. I really didn't think I would get to rush. Especially with the Zeta Beta Gammas. Since I'm a high school drop-out and they are big into academics, they were super iffy about letting me in. See, all the Greek houses look at your academic records like your GPA, high school accomplishments, club memberships, and stuff like that. Since I only have my GED, I don't have any of that, but some of the houses are letting me rush anyway.

I'm starting to feel part of something bigger now. I hope this is the right start to my new life. I'm trying to make better choices. Something good should come out of this. I will be part of a family within a bigger organization. It seems like I'm on the right track. I'm hoping I get in good with the Zeta Bs. They are my favorite girls so far, and I see big possibilities!

Week Three – College

OK. SO, I may have jumped the gun. I am pledging the Zeta Bs now, but no one told me that there are *so* many rules to a sorority. I mean, look, no offense. I don't want to offend anyone who has been so kind to me. But no one is gonna tell me what I have to wear on Monday or Wednesday or any day, for that matter. So no, my new friends, I will not be wearing matching pink polo shirts and minis skirts with you. Ever. For the love of all that is holy. Aren't we a little old to be all matchy-matchy? I'm just not into it. I'm more like an original, one- of-a kind, uniquely dressed vibe. Sorry, but I'm just gonna keep wearing my old music T-shirts and daisy dukes with my Justin boots. And my tie-dye. And my baggy old-man sweaters. You do you, though. I'm not judging. I just don't want to do all the required dressing-alike. It's a lot.

Also, I'm not gonna be told which bars I can or cannot go to or who I can hang out with. I mean, who does that? Seriously. The "we all have to look and act exactly the same" mindset is definitely different and I cannot keep doing it. I already have some great friends that aren't in Greek life here. They were my very first friends, and I'm not gonna just ditch them like these girls want me to. I also already have my music and clothing styles. I don't need to be dictated to and made to be someone I'm not or do things that I don't want to. And I already know how to have a good time. In fact, I think they should take some notes from me on that last one. They are a little bit uptight.

To be honest, the Greek idea of a good time on this campus is so lame. I've been sneaking into cool frat parties since I was fourteen. These small campus houses just suck. Their Greek houses are cringy. They are inexpensive and tiny compared to the enormous mansions on Greek row in my hometown. This week has become disappointing. I'm just gonna keep being the real me. They can take it or leave it.

It's suddenly clicking that paying hundreds of dollars a month in dues to them for me to *not* hang out with these girls makes zero sense. I'm wasting a lot of money trying to join this organization. Why? It's obviously not my jam. Side note: Dad was pissed about the cost of becoming a pledge anyway. He said, and I quote, "That's a lot of money that I could be spending on Jan." I'll give it to him. He was right about this one. I don't fit into a mold, and I never will. This isn't going to work out, so I think I'm gonna have to drop out of rush week and hang with my good ole GDIs. That stands for G*@ Da*% Independents. (I won't use that word. I was raised in church, after all.)

Anyway, my two options for fun activities this afternoon when I'm out of class are to go watch a bunch of girls I don't know from all the sorority houses play flag football in the humidity and heat for hours with the frat guys the sorority says I have to hang out with. (Yuck, in case you didn't get that vibe already.) Or go drink ice cold beer in the air conditioning and play pool with people I do know and who, heaven forbid, prefer the ZBGs listen to *rap* music. Gasp! The more I get to know the GDIs, the more I love them. It's not rocket science. I will always take option two. The GDIs are my amigos. That's how I roll.

I'm definitely more of an independent kind of gal. With all these social activities and time spent hanging out with new people, I still haven't found love or anything even remotely close to it. That bums me out. However, I never said I haven't already screwed a couple of random, hot guys here for my research. Don't judge. I mean, what's a girl to do? I'll just have to crack open an ice-cold brewski, hope I don't scratch on the eight ball, and toast to eventually finding love. Cheers, amigos!

Week Four – College

I OFFICIALLY DROPPED OUT of the sorority. Man, were they ever pissed! I honestly never thought of that. I guess a pledge dropping out never happens. Leave it to me to do something different and unexpected. I'm not sure if that's a good or bad trait. Anyway, word on the street is that once I quit, a wave of others started dropping out. Who knew? I guess I'm a leader in disguise. I'm just being me, and I won't ever apologize for that. Needless to say, the Beta Z girls now turn up their noses when they see me on campus. Funny thing about it, the Greek guys are all still friendly. They have no drama. (Also, I'm still friendly with them, and who knows? I might become their next sexual opportunity if one of them plays their cards right. That's not rocket science either.) Whatever. Adios bitchachos! I feel great about my decision. Greek life definitely was not for me. I realized it and moved along. Side note: I'm not going to pay actual money, *lots* of real money for friends.

In other news, I am not doing great in my classes. I am trying though. I really, really am. Apparently, I didn't learn a lot of things that I needed to know for college because I dropped out of high school. I'm trying my best and just winging it. There's nothing else to do but see how it goes. As of now, the only class I'm passing is English, and it's only week four! I'm in big trouble here. My roomie and my friends are trying to help me catch up, but it's not going so great. After I attempt to do my homework every day, I go drink some beer with my friends to relax and just try not to think about it. The bars never card any of the girls here, either, because where the girls go, the guys follow. That being said, the bars want me inside. It's good for business. At least I have that going for me.

Week Five – College

WELL, I'M IN tutoring because I'm hard-core flunking out of everything but English, and even in that, I'm only hanging on by a thread. I have a D. I called to talk to Dad about it, and he was in a drunken, mumbling slurry. He just screamed raging, undiscernible words (which I'm sure were profanities and insults) at me. I also told him that I dropped out of Greek life. I thought maybe that would calm him down since it would save lots of money, but he was too drunk to care. Honestly, I don't think he even understood what I was saying. He was hammered. Then Jan grabbed the phone from him and was trying to talk to me like a mom or something. What a total joke. She was all "Sweetie, blah blah blah this" and "Honey, blah blah blah that." I told her I could tell she was drunk too and that I'm not her sweetie or honey. She made a big sucking noise, like taking in a huge gulp of air, followed by silence. Then she screamed at me to "fuck off, you little bitch" and hung up.

I can't keep taking this emotional roller coaster ride of hate and abuse when all I am doing is trying my best. Since Dad and Jan are the only home I have to call, I'll wait a few weeks and phone again even though I know better. Then when I do, it's the same awful result. I don't want to ever call again, *again.* Eventually, I break down and try to call again, hoping for a healthier result. Instead, the conversation is never good. Ever. And who else do I have? I'm stuck in a vicious cycle. This is exactly why I'm determined to always be on the lookout for love, for my man. I have got to figure out my life, a new life. If I can just find love somewhere, I can create my own family and a home full of love. I can't go live back at Dad's house. Not ever. This is all very depressing and heavy, so I think I'm gonna go to my favorite bar, Tropicana. Tonight is dollar pitchers. They play great dance music, and the sorority girls refuse to go there because it's not classy enough for them. Perfect. A lot of sketchy and fun stuff goes on there. They also play the best dance music and have the cheapest drinks. It's a win-win for me.

I look at the clock, and it's barely two p.m. Luckily for me, that's what time Tropicana opens. Unluckily, all my friends are still in class. Unlike most girls my age, I'm cool with going to a bar by myself. My friends and I always meet up there on Wednesdays, so they'll show sooner or later. I check my makeup in the mirror, grab my wallet, and take off, walking the few short blocks it takes to get there. Inside, I immediately feel at ease. The bartender knows me. That's not really something to brag about, it's just the truth. As I walk over and hop on a stool at the end of the bar, he finishes wiping the counter top off.

Looking up, he says, "Hey. What can I get ya?" I order an ice-cold pitcher of beer for the bargain price of one dollar along with a shot of Jim Beam. "Starting early today."

"Yep." A whole pitcher of beer is a lot for one-hundred-pound me to drink, but I can handle it. Plus, it's not like I'm in any rush to drink it. I pour some Coors into my frost covered glass and take a swig. It's so good. Then, I shoot the Jim and feel the burn all the way down the back of my throat. *Aaah. Delicious. Just what I needed.*

The place is almost pitch black except a few dim spotlights around the empty dance floor. Fake palm trees are everywhere, and they have a handwritten list of tropical drink specials on the chalk board. The bar was silent when I came in, but now, the music is turned on, the bass vibrating the walls and floor. When it's pumping, you can barely hear yourself think. It's great. I sit, perched up at the bar, drinking and chain smoking, singing and swaying to the beat. I don't know how long it's been, but a couple of my friends eventually show up. We dance and do a bunch of shots. My pitcher of beer is long gone. With the buzz, I feel much better since my call with Dad. Dancing and music always puts me in a great mood. I'm good on the drinking for now. I made up a sobriety test for myself a long time ago to decide this. Step one is to walk to the bathroom. Step two is to go into a stall and attempt to unzip my pants without falling over. Step three (obviously) is to go pee. While I pee, I notice if the stall spins. If so, no more drinking. Step four is after peeing, if the stall is not spinning, can I zip my pants up on the first try? If so, I'm still good to drink. If not, stop drinking immediately. It's my own unspoken rule for myself that I never want to be too drunk in public just so that I stay aware and safe. Well, today, the stall is indeed spinning, and I can barely zip my pants back up. That means I am done drinking for now, but I will just keep dancing until last call.

Our group is all mingling, dancing, and laughing, having a great time and minding our own business when, out of nowhere, some girl comes pushing her way through our circle and dumps a glass of beer right over my friend Tyrone's head in the middle of the dance floor. Then she just walks off. What the hell? I'm pissed. Tyrone, now shocked and dripping wet, is a very mellow, friendly guy. He's not aggressive or dramatic, and I do not like anyone disrespecting me or any of my friends. In fact, I will not tolerate it. Tyrone is actually from a really poor family, and he is dressed in his very best clothes tonight because he is supposed to be meeting up with a girl he's interested in. He is drenched now, and his outfit for the evening is ruined, which adds to my fury. I stop dancing and ask him what the hell that was all about. He tells me that he and the beer-dumping girl went on a date a few weeks prior, and he didn't think they clicked, so he never called her again. That's it. "I got this," I tell him, fuming.

Pressing through the crowd now up at the bar, I order another entire pitcher of beer. Carrying it by the handle, I search the crowd. It takes some time, but I locate the girl on the packed dance floor, laughing and living it up with her girlfriends. I walk up behind her and tap her on the shoulder. As she turns around, I pour the entire pitcher of beer over her head. "I will beat you at your own game, sweetie. Leave my friends alone!" I yell at her over the music. As I'm yelling and holding the now empty plastic pitcher over her head in one hand, someone behind me grabs my arms and holds them together as I am simultaneously scooped up by the crotch. I'm picked right up off the floor, dangling like a kid on the high end of a teeter totter with an unknown and very large hand holding me up by my lady bits.

A man tells me to calm down as I am screaming and flailing for him to let me go. I can barely hear over the music. The now sopping wet, beer-drenched girl takes the second I'm restrained to smack me in the face as my arms are pinned behind me. I am yelling at the large man, who turns out to be the bouncer, to put me down and still wiggling and fighting him as much as I can. She's standing there laughing, because she smacked me. I rear back in an attempt to head butt the bouncer. It doesn't quite work, but one of my arms slips free, so I twist violently and quickly out and away from his grip.

Jumping to the ground, I lunge at her, punching her in the face and jumping on top of her as we roll around, screaming insults, fighting on the sticky wooden floor. There is hair pulling, yelling, hitting, clawing, and slapping, and now everyone in the bar is watching. A circle has grown around us, and people are cheering. My knees are burning, getting skinned up from the rough floor, but I ignore it. I'm in a rage like I haven't felt in months. More bouncers gather to help the one who lost control of me, and together, they grab both of us and pull us apart.

Catching a glimpse of my friends who all look shocked because they don't know about my scrappy past, I smile and wink as I am forcibly moved from inside the bar to the sidewalk outside and told not to come back tonight. I don't care. I inspect my arms and legs, feel my head and face, then lick my lower lip, which tastes like blood and feels a bit puffy. My only real injuries are large, dirty scrapes from the floor on my knees, elbows, and one of my arms as well as some pretty busted-up knuckles. Good. I shake myself off, roll my shoulders back, and rotate my head and neck to the right and left. I am missing one of my big, fake silver hoop earrings. Oh well. Nothing but the knuckles on my right hand and both knees hurt. Great. The adrenaline is wearing off. I bet my hair looks like crap. *I'm proud of you for standing up for your friend*, I think as I walk back to the dorm to get some sleep. *Screw that girl.* I half expect the cops to show up later, but they never do. All in all, I'd still say it was another great night out.

Week Six – College

IT ONLY TOOK me one more week to officially flunk all my classes. Congratulations to me for being a total akademic loser. (See what I did there with the *k*? Ha! I'm trying to keep my sense of humor about all this.) I'm totally screwed, and major panic is setting in. My plan for this new college life is unraveling around me faster than a kite string twirling in a tornado. So many people have tried to help, even tutors. By the time I realized how clueless I was, it was too late to fix my grades, no matter how hard I tried. Something in my brain is just not tracking with college requirements and how everything in the college system works. If I felt like a failure and a joke before, I feel like an even worse one now. I feel extra stupid because it never crossed my mind that I would not actually be able to succeed in my plan. I never in a million years thought I might fail. As a high school drop- out,

I just didn't know what I didn't know, and my grades quickly dropped beyond any hope of redemption.

The only thing I can do to temporarily make myself feel better about the entire situation is to get drunk, dance, and hopefully find a hot guy to hang with. It's not like I have anything to lose. I will say that certain people are giving me a new respect on campus. Word seems to have gotten around about the fight at the Tropicana. Now the sorority girls are back to smiling artificially at me if we accidentally make eye contact. I obviously make them nervous when they find themselves around me. My friends say how awesome it was that I stood up for Tyrone. He thinks it was awesome too. I'm not so sure about that. I was really trying to leave my scrappy days in the past. I'm a bit disappointed in myself in more ways than one. I don't want my future to include fighting.

This is what happens. There I was, minding my own business and trying to turn over a new leaf when I was tempted to act like my old self. If I'm honest, I did enjoy the fight at the time a little bit, but I know it wasn't right. Surely, the good Lord must have better plans for me. I know that He does not endorse my drunkenness, fighting, or screwing. And I definitely know that *Baptist* Jesus most certainly does not. From what I've witnessed, it seems to me that Baptist Jesus is more strict than Catholic Jesus, but I'm not certain of that. I'm just saying that I'm running out of options here, and I cannot just sit around. I'm a high energy go-getter. And I need something to go my way. Soon.

My stress level is through the roof, and I need to release some tension. That's exactly why the fight felt so good. I'm still trying to change things in my life, and I've also decided that I'm not calling home anymore. Dad and Jan either don't answer the phone at all or pick up and start to cuss me out. College isn't working. Family isn't working. Finding love isn't working. My whole life isn't really working. It's time for me to make another new plan. Lord, help me.

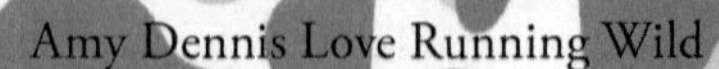
Amy Dennis Love Running Wild

Week Seven – College

OK, I HAVE thought and thought. Here it is, my new plan. I'm going to head back to my hometown in a few weeks where I've already lined up a full-time job at the Burger Shack. It's not great, but it's a start, and I will get to live on my own doing it. I'm scrimping and saving up enough money to pay for a tiny apartment and all the deposits and related costs. Full disclosure, to pay for all the up-front costs of moving, I have just started stripping.

I am not proud of this type of work. However, I am proud that I found a job. At least it's only a couple of nights a week. I'm working at a newly opened juice bar. The term "juice bar," for those who don't know, means that the dancers, me included, will be totally naked while dancing because no alcohol is served. I did not exactly realize that until after I got hired. Anyhow, I ended up here because I heard an ad on the radio that they were hiring immediately and the commercial said the pay was "outstanding." I just wandered in to check the place out since I'd never even been inside a strip club before. I decided that a random Monday around one p.m. would be as good a time as any to go. When I asked the bouncer about it, he went and got a guy from the back office. He was super sketchy looking and probably fifty- five with greasy brown hair and a porn stache. He was also wearing some dark-tinted, seventies-looking pimp glasses and a cheap purple silk shirt unbuttoned down to almost his stomach. He had multiple (probably fake) gold chains around his neck and was chewing on a soggy-tipped cigar. He eyeballed me, looking me up and down in a very obvious and perverted way, and then just asked me if I could dance. I said, "Well, of course, or I wouldn't be here" while I tried to maintain eye contact so I'd appear confident. He totally creeped me out.

Then, he just kept standing there, undressing me with his eyes, and said, "Dance." So I danced, fully clothed, to whatever music was already playing in the background. And that was it. I got the job. I'm pretty sure I heard him low key growl while I was performing. *Yuck*. Anyway, the place is on the edge of town, and it's called "The Lucky Beaver." I. Know. The patrons are so excited that the joint is finally open that it's been packed every night. I've been making more money in one night here than I'd make at a job in two weeks anywhere else. Honestly, I have to still pep talk myself into going in every night. I'm doing it because I'm desperate. It usually gets easier as the night goes on.

I go in to work early, wearing skimpy, cute clothes, of course. That's pretty much how I dress all the time anyway. I wander casually around, checking out the evening's clientele, and try to get into the vibe of the place for the night since it's always different. I flit around from seat to seat, table to table, acting confident, laughing, smiling, and joking (while I still have clothes on) although I am nauseated every night with nerves. I talk up the guys sitting in the VIP area and flirt with any other guys who look like they might have big bucks to spend freely. Interestingly, I quickly learned that truckers come with lots more cash-o-la than you would think.

I focus on anyone who seems especially interested in talking with me specifically or on the regulars who I know will pay me well for a little extra attention. If I happen to overhear that it's someone's birthday or special occasion like a bachelor party, I make sure to acknowledge it with a "Happy birthday, hon" or "Congratulations, sweetie. She sure is getting a good one in you!" I always give a little extra attention and boob shaking for the special guest. That small eye for detail works like a charm every single time. Men love having their ego stroked almost as much as their you-know-what. The guys celebrating are always in a great mood and are here to party and spend without limit. I do keep an eye out for the creeps and steer clear of them, no matter how much cash they dish out to the other girls. I strut around, sure, but I'm terrified and quivering inside.

This is still all very new to me, being one of these hot, buck-naked girls. I give just enough effort and TLC when I arrive that it sets me up to get great tips long before I ever have to go up on stage. My goal is to get the patrons to adore me while also spending the very least amount of time possible naked. This is what I call my strategic marketing plan. The goal is to make them love me and want me before I dance. If

I spend extra time *clothed* with them before my shift, maybe they will desire me more. I make them feel emotionally attached to me because I make them feel special. Thus, they pay me more overall for a shorter time of nakedness. They are there to watch our naked parts gyrating, but a few mind games won't hurt my pay. I will 100 percent try to manipulate the situation while my clothes remain on.

I told you before that I'm hot. I wasn't lying. Not to be cocky, but I am by far the hottest girl at the club. The guys enjoy talking to me, and hell, they practically drool on me even when I walk in the place. I wish I didn't have to dance nude, but I do, so I just keep telling myself that all this cash for my future is worth it. This is a stepping stone. It's not forever. At least, I really love dancing in general; that's a little bit of a silver lining. A person always needs to find their silver lining. If I close my eyes when I dance, I sort of forget where I am for a few minutes. That helps too. I think about how much better work would be if they allowed us to have at least bikini bottoms on. That would be amazing. I dream about one day having a paid-off car and a safe, cozy house. I dream about wearing a sexy outfit, dancing at home only for the man I will find to love. In my opinion, my humongous boobs are way too saggy without wearing a top. But the guys at the club obviously think differently. So drink your juice and make it rain for these ta-tas, fellas!

Before I go on stage, I smoke weed. It's the only time I do. I just take a couple of tokes from a joint to help me chill out. And I drink just enough booze, a shot or two of tequila, to make me feel like I am invincible. Several of the other girls do pills, coke, and other drugs, but that's crazy. That's way too dangerous. I'm not trying to die from taking a pill mixed with who knows what or have a heart attack from coke, much less shoot up. Hell, no. No, thank you, ma'am. I will pass on all of that absolute nonsense.

I keep my thin silky little robe on and belted around the waist and wear my fuzzy slippers until the very last possible second. I will never understand how lots of the other girls prance around in the back naked as jay birds, like it's nothing. I always feel super shy even in the dim lights. When I dance, I have to keep my eyes closed as much as possible to keep my nerves at bay as I gyrate on the cold pole. When I do open my eyes, I quickly scan the darkened room for whoever looks like they have the most money and/or regulars who I know pay well.

The room's energy is constantly shifting, so I have to pay attention. I try to gauge who is most into my performance and who seems to be having the most overall fun. I have to watch to see if anyone in the crowd is getting angry or if anyone is being stalkerish or pervy. I make some eye contact with men as I dance their way, but I hate the eye contact because they always break it to look at my body like I'm a piece of meat. That makes me want to throw up. Also, eye contact is intimate, and I am *not* trying to be intimate with any of these guys. There is a fine line between *some* eye contact and *too much* eye contact, and it is very hard to gauge because it all depends on the man.

I just try to keep my mind on the money I will have at the end of the night as the eyes of the men devour me. *Focus on the dollars, focus on the dollars,* I repeat over and over in my mind. I concentrate all my efforts on where I think the money is going to come from for the night, and I usually guess pretty well. I'm good at reading the crowd, and only the very, very top spenders ever get a glimpse at my, uh, private privates. Even though I'm new at this, I immediately found ways to dance and be sexy without just spreading my legs. A lot of the girls do *freaky* stuff. Not me. I'm as prude as a stripper can possibly be. I know what you're thinking. I already told you I'm a slut. So who cares? I do. It's a matter of what I *choose* to do and what I *have* to do. I also refuse to do sexual favors for patrons. I know those girls make way more money, but I don't care. I won't do that. Is it worse for me to do it for free outside of work or not do it at work even for money? That is one of my life's tough questions. These thoughts keep me up at night.

Weeks Eight to Sixteen – College

I'M NOT BOTHERING to attend classes anymore since I'm officially flunking out. Like, for real. It's solid F's across the board with no coming back. I've still got a place to sleep in the dorm until the semester is over. I mean, it's already paid for, so why not? I'll be moving back home pretty soon to my own soon-to-be-rented place. With the job at the club, I still make really good money, and I'm ready to get the hell out of here. I strip and sleep, strip and sleep. Most of the students don't really hang out with me anymore. I am definitely seeing the difference between being a college student and, well, not being one. It's actually kind of lonely at the moment. I sleep when they are all in class, and I'm working when they are partying. I'm on my own weird, isolated schedule between the two worlds of college life and adulting. I don't quite fit anywhere. Again.

Sometimes, I see guys from campus at the club, and that's just weird. I feel like a total skank. I try not to get up on stage if any of them walk in. It's embarrassing. Like I'm a failure. I guess that *is* what my F's stand for. Dad was so pissed when he found out about those F's, slamming down the phone when I called and told him. We haven't spoken since. I'm still looking for love and not finding shit. I'm over everything. It's not like I'm gonna find love at the strip club. Let's be real. At least I've got some money saved up in the bank and some cash stashed in a secret jar that looks like it's Jiffy peanut butter. I'm just hanging in there, biding my time and wondering how I ended up in a mess again. I really did try my best to create a better life for myself. This whole thing is a bummer. Well, I gave it the old college try. Ha. I try to always find an upside to my story, and I guess an upside is that I am drinking *a lot* more juice than I ever have before. Because you know, work. Juice bar. I guess that means I'm getting lots of vitamin C, so at least I don't have to worry about coming down with scurvy. Whoopee!

Now: Luca

I GUESS BY NOW, I should have introduced myself. Hey. My name's Luca. I've always felt out of place, and as you know, it's been pounded into my head since I was very young that I'm not wanted. My parents swear I'm unlovable, and I still can't figure out what I did to make them hate me so much. They've just always said that I'm a screw up and a mistake. At barely eighteen, I'm apparently still too messed up to be loved. I'm not perfect, I get it. But they have drilled every possible flaw and failure of mine into my head for as long as I can remember. Their negativity constantly rattles around in my brain although I do my best to fight it off.

According to them, I'm not special, not worth anyone's time, and definitely not worth loving. Hell, I'm barely tolerable if you ask Dad. I'm sure he blames me because Mom left a while back. She never could really stomach being around me. Some days, I don't think I'm as bad as they say. On really good days, I start to think that I'm unique, funny, and even a little bit smart. At the very least, I'm not boring. And I'm not a total idiot, so that's something. A battle is raging every single day in my head. I try as hard as I can to remain positive about myself. Usually, I manage to stay convinced that if I just keep plowing ahead and doing my best, life will work out, and everything will end up ok. I'm hoping I'll find love, sooner rather than later. I'm fed up with being alone.

I've tried all the normal things that people do to find love. At least I think I have. I've also done some pretty wild shit. And guess what? Here I am. All by my lonesome. I mean, I have some people I could call friends, but they're more like casual acquaintances. Drinking buddies. You know the type. People who are always down to party but are nowhere to be found when you really need a shoulder to cry on or need help with something. I feel like who I really am is an invisible loner. Not by choice. No one sees the pain in my soul. I've got all these overwhelming emotions inside, and no one has ever cared enough to ask about them. I have no one to rely on but myself. And there's no place that I truly fit in. No one gets me. I have never felt truly safe in my entire life, especially not at home. That's why I'm always on edge, ready for anything.

These days, I don't trust anyone. I've been hurt too much. So here I am. Flunking out of college with crushed dreams and learning quickly how to strip. The only positive thing, if you want to call it that, is the cash I now have in the bank (and stashed all over my dorm room) from stripping. I'm not sure how positive that really is. It's just not a total negative. And it's definitely something I need to keep surviving. I'm a loser and alone. Still. Sorry about my whining. I'm just sick of it all.

I expected my family to love me. They didn't. I expected to find friends to love me. Most of them were either mooches who were just using me or two-faced. I thought for sure one of my many boyfriends would love me. Nope. All they did was lie, screw me, cheat, and disappear.

I even finally, in total desperation, tried going back to church to find love. I was raised in church like most people from the Midwest, so going back to it as some kind of last resort made sense. Turns out, that may have been one of my worst decisions. I had high hopes that God's people would show me some type of love. Surely, I thought, *they* would welcome me, a wayward daughter, with open arms. The church proclaims to be there for us: the misfits, sinners, and prodigals. Sadly, they were the cruelest bunch of all. My discovery of this was disheartening.

I had conjured an image up in my mind of a warm greeting when I arrived in my Sunday best as a guest. The welcome you always picture and pray you'll find at church. I envisioned showing up and being welcomed by a kind, chubby lady who looked like Mrs. Clause. She would be smiling from ear to ear and would smell like sugar cookies and baby powder. She'd insist on giving me a hug while calling me "honey" or "sweetheart" and tell me how glad she was that I was "finally home." Then she'd usher me right in to sit beside her, her soft grandmotherly arm draped lovingly around me on the second pew.

I honestly didn't think that idea was too far-fetched. Everywhere you turn, churches are inviting people to come check them out and "be our guest" with their flyers, billboards, and radio commercials. It took me a lot of time, like weeks and weeks, to finally work up the nerve to walk inside, you know? I am one of the church's lost sheep, so I always feel like a sinner and a loser. I figured I would feel even more like one *in* church around all those holy people, and that does not seem like it would be an enjoyable experience, obviously. But they say that "Everyone is welcome" or "Come as you are," and I felt like I needed a change so I finally went with a belly full of nerves and Saturday night's cheap vodka.

I'm sorry to report that I did not feel welcome nor did I find the love of God or of anyone there. All I found was more shame and judgement. I've had unsweetened tea that was sweeter than those people. I think that tells you all you need to know. I mean, really, if you don't practice what you preach, what's the point in preaching at all? I was raised hearing that Jesus loves *every* sinner. I thought that meant I'd be included. I left that service with more sadness in my soul than I'd had going in. I'm used to people letting me down. Now, I feel let down by church and God too. *That's* a hard pill to swallow.

I'm just so tired of looking for acceptance. I'm trying my hardest to find peace. I'm trying to do the right things. I want to settle down and create a loving home with someone. I need to find out where I fit in. Really, I'm just doing my best to try to be lovable. "Lovable Luca." That's what I keep calling myself. It has a nice ring to it. Love is all I want, but I can't seem to find it, no matter what I do. I keep thinking that if I just keep calling myself "Lovable Luca," it might come true one day. So I keep looking for love the best I know how everywhere I go. And I guess looking for love is how I ended up standing here, staring down the barrel of Jack's shotgun. Pregnant.

Then: Luca

DEEP DOWN, I had never quite given up hope that someone out there would love me. The fact that I am not loved has been screamed in my face, mainly by my mom. Dad joined in too when he was drinking, which turned out to be more and more often over the years. The women in Mom's church circle would never have believed it had I dared whisper the truth of Mom's daily drunken state, so I just kept my mouth shut.

Mom lived for years and years with an unhappiness brought on by something I could not see or understand. As I said earlier, one day, on a random Tuesday, she finally left Dad and me for who knows where. She just never came back. Dad and I had both known that Mom was very melancholy. But only I knew that she secretly liked to get hammered on gas station wine while I was at school and Dad was at work. I really think she thought I didn't know.

The day my mom left, a tiny piece of my heart became irreparably broken. I felt even more unlovable in that single minute than I ever had before because she had now officially deserted me. I was abandoned. I became a half orphan in my mind. Now, I had only Dad left, and I wondered if Mom leaving was my fault. After a few minutes of standing on the sidewalk feeling numb and kind of lost, I scurried inside the house. The tall, cheap black plastic kitchen trash can was tipped over. Wine bottles and other garbage were strewn about on the old oak-planked floor. Upstairs, there were more bottles. Some, half empty, sat on the dresser with their screw tops missing. I picked one up and took a swig as I surveyed what was once a pristinely kept room. A couple more bottles, also drained, were knocked over, their lips oozing remnants of cheap, crimson wine. The ruby red liquid spread like blood from a severed artery across the old black-and-white-tiled bathroom. A Waterford Crystal goblet that used to be my Grandmother's was smashed to bits, its pointed shards glistening in the afternoon light like the dust of diamonds.

Apparently, Mom had hurled it against the mirror, which now bore a large splintering crack straight down the middle. Interestingly, I caught a brief glimpse of my reflection, and the crack in the image was right over my heart. A flicker of sadness went through me. This was no time for thoughts or feelings like that. I quickly looked away. I guess drinking Boone's Farm from a Waterford chalice instead of her usual brown paper bag was Mom's last hurrah. What an interesting choice. Maybe she was trying to leave with a little class. Ha. This is what I do. I joke to myself when life is rough.

Anyway, the house was a mess. Back in the kitchen, dirty dishes were piled up high in the sink. Dusty, torn boxes Mom must have dragged from the attic were left strewn in the hall. Old unwashed, stained items of Mom's clothing had been thrown about and were heaped in piles on the floor. Photo albums were scattered and opened on the coffee table in the living room as if she had been reminiscing. However, no photos had been removed for her to take when she left. Apparently, images of the family were not treasured memories to her.

I hurried to clean the mess up before Dad got home. When he arrived, I was nervous to tell him the news. I knew I had to, though, so I took a deep breath and then told him as gently as I could that Mom had deserted us. He didn't say a thing. He just got a sad, faraway look in his eyes. His shoulders slumped, and then, stuffing his hands into the pockets of his overalls, he dejectedly walked onto the front porch and stared toward the neighbors' pasture for a long, long time, not seeming to focus on anything in particular.

When Dad came back into the house hours later, it was dark, and he went straight to the cupboard, pulling out a bottle of whiskey, right in front of me instead of trying to hide it like usual. He guzzled shot after shot until he was obliterated. Only then did he flop down in his old brown creaky La-Z-Boy chair, which was pocked with cigarette burns. He started sobbing like a baby. Holding his head in his hands, he cried so hard that his shoulders shook up and down like a bobber when the fish are biting.

Dad was never the same after that. He started to drown his heartbreak in whiskey on a more public and routine basis.

He also stayed constantly angry with me. I think this was due to his new-found daily drunkenness. We never talked about Mom's leaving, but I knew he blamed me for everything. So life just moved on but got worse. Dad was quick to get a girlfriend, and she moved right in to take mom's place. She tried to, that is. Daddy said this was to help raise me, but I had just turned seventeen by then, and I didn't need any of her raising. I knew she was only there to cook, clean, and satisfy him. Jan was pale and really skinny with stringy brown hair and bad skin that she tried to hide beneath five pounds of cheap makeup. Jan had what I like to call stupid eyes. They were just a teeny bit too far apart from each other and never quite focused on what she was looking at. When she looked at me, it was as if she couldn't quite grasp any concept and was constantly thinking, Duuuh." You know, like the light's on, but no one's home. I thought maybe she was inbred, but I had no way to find out for sure.

As slow as she was, Jan made it clear that she did not want me around. It was my guess she was a lot closer to my age than Dad's. And she was a real peach. Not a week after she moved in, she started in on me, telling me when Dad wasn't around that I was worthless and other endearing comments like that. What a huge crock of shit that was, and I told her so.

She definitely wasn't any kinder to me than Mom had been. I hated her and tried to steer clear of her as much as possible. She really made it a point, though, to get up in my face any chance she got. (When Dad wasn't around, of course.) He couldn't understand my seething rage toward her. She honestly thought she could treat me however she pleased.

One day, she wouldn't back off, even though I'd already told her politely to stop screaming at me several times. I'd had enough of her trash talk. She just kept blathering on and on at me, and I snapped. The next thing I knew, I had punched her right in the mouth, and we got into a full-blown cat fight right there on the front porch. I'm not proud of what I did. Oh hell, who am I kidding? Yes. I am. I am proud of what I did. I finally stood up for myself and beat Jan's ass to a bloody pulp. Go, me!

The neighbors called the cops. Luckily, neither of us went to jail. I honestly think the officer just felt sorry for me about the whole situation. He very kindly showed compassion and gave me a much-needed break. I was appreciative. I hardly ever get a break. Although the fight upset Dad, I didn't care because Jan (and her big mouth) left me alone after that. Our disdain for each other was blatantly obvious to anyone around, and Dad was becoming more intolerable by the day.

By this point, I was getting really tired of people talking to me and treating me like I was a problem and a piece of crap in my own house. Several other people were telling me that everything going wrong in life was my fault too. From my school principal, to kids in town, and of course, the church people. Pretty much everywhere I went, I heard that I was no good. I was a "troublemaker," a "slut," and a "liar." I needed to behave and obey. These folks had no specific reasons to call me any of these names, mind you. It was just the town gossip mill, which I'm sure started in Mom's gossipy prayer group. Prayer is prayer, and gossip is gossip. The Lord knows which is which.

Of course, I am the first to admit that I did do the average crazy teenage stuff, but nothing, in my opinion, to support all the name calling. At least at the beginning and especially not by nosey, holier-than-thou adults. Eventually, I did turn into quite a scrappy little tramp. And looking back, I can pinpoint the fighting side of me coming to a head that day with Jan. Until then, I didn't know my own strength or how good it felt to stand up for myself and win. After that, anyone who disrespected me was fair game. However, I never was a liar, so it really pissed me off when people called me one. Maybe I just have Daddy issues or Mommy issues or both. Who knows? Your guess is as good as mine.

Even with all the crap being said about me, I still felt a weird, tingling hope that love was out there, somewhere. Every day, I thought it might be waiting for me, right around the next corner, if I just kept going. Surely one man somewhere would want me to be his. I really hoped so, because I felt like a specific part of me had always been missing. My soul felt like how it looks when you are putting a jigsaw puzzle together and you're down to that very last piece that fits exactly right. *That* was the piece I was looking for. And I was pretty sure it was heart-shaped. I wasn't looking for a friendship kind of love from girls or to be the favorite pet of a teacher or boss. I never needed that. I just wanted him. The one. My guy, who would love me, no matter what. Then we could create our own sweet life, safe and sound. It would be peaceful and wonderful. Then I would have a home and, most importantly, I would *finally* be loved. I was just trying to be "Lovable Luca." And I just had to believe that my man was out there.

Now: Luca

I AM FREAKING OUT. Jack is shoving the end of a loaded shotgun in my face. He's standing as still as a statue, staring me down like a rabid animal. Drunk. Yelling. This is *not* how I envisioned my announcement going at all. I've been dreaming up baby names. I've been wondering how I would tell him. I was a little nervous as anyone in my situation would be. But I was never worried. No. I was never worried about his response. How blind and totally stupid of me.

Jack has told me for months and months that he loves me. That we are going to get married. That I'm his woman. He has never said one unkind word or been unloving in any way. I assumed he would be happy. He is not. He. Is. Furious. And he has me cornered between the wall of the living room and the dark, narrow, wood-paneled hallway that leads to his office in the back of his house. His brown eyes that are usually so soft and full of kindness have turned to beads of steel. They are full of disgust. The rage is rolling off him.

My plan was to come here to his normal weekend keg party and hang out like always. Then later, in a private moment, I would tell him our exciting news. The exact wording options I could use have been running through my mind for a couple of weeks. "You are going to be a dad!" Or maybe, "Guess who's pregnant?" with a cute smile and a quick rub of my flat stomach. He would be overjoyed, and we would start planning our future immediately. Together. As a family.

Was this pregnancy unplanned? Yes. Were we careful? Yes. Somehow, I had figured that because we were in love and had already been talking about marriage, the little bun in the oven would be an unexpected but good surprise. That's where I got it wrong. I am figuring it out right now as events unfold. His body is rigid and shaking, and his savage glare radiates with intense hatred. And every ounce of it is directed at me.

It starts the second I walk through his front door and don't take the beer Jack tries to hand me. He tilts his head and squints, looking at me with suspicion, giving me a quick once over as Metallica blasts from the stereo. "Here," he tries again, shoving the cold cup at me. I push it away casually. "No thanks. I'm good." He knows something's off. He slams the red, disposable cup down onto an end table. Beer sloshes over the top, wetting his hand. Jack doesn't seem to notice. Grabbing a crumpled pack of Marlboro Reds from his shirt pocket, he taps out a cigarette. Then fishing around in his Levi 501's for his cherished Zippo, he finds it and lights up with the flip and click of its metallic top, never averting his gaze from me. Shoving the lighter back into his jeans, Jack picks up his own plastic cup of beer, taking a long swig. His questioning eyes focus on me in a steady and chilling gaze. The look reminds me of a wolf stalking its prey. A flutter of nerves suddenly flops around in my chest. Although the living room is full of people, I hardly know them. These are his friends, not mine. I'm quickly becoming more and more anxious. A barely perceptible undercurrent of danger is flowing from him directly to me. My primal instincts are now on high alert.

Everyone else is partying it up, drinking, smoking weed, dancing and totally unaware that this moment is quickly becoming the start of a nightmare for me. Party goers, oblivious, over on the couch start shrieking and clapping. They are so rowdy even over the song "Janie's Got a Gun" blaring full blast from the living room speakers. Their ruckus snatches my attention. Some dude is snorting lines of coke off a mirror on the coffee table, and everyone is cheering him on. *Great crowd*, I sarcastically think. My mind flips back to Jack. Although it feels like hours have passed, it's only been a few seconds. I don't know what Jack is about to say or do. Sweat breaks out on my palms. I swallow, trying to get rid of the sour taste that is suddenly in the back of my throat.

Jack is thinking, calculating his next move, his expression changing from "happy to see me" when I walked in two minutes ago to fury faster than I could blink. He roughly nudges me with his elbow down the dark hall. "Get into my office, *now*!" he growls. "You're pregnant, aren't you?" I never even get the chance to say yes. He knows. I obey his gruff order and start walking slowly toward the office, thinking about what I can do. My mind races. Apparently, I'm not moving fast enough for him. Blocking the hallway with his body and shoving me with his empty hand the remaining few steps into the office, he chugs the rest of his beer, crumpling the cup with one hand and throwing it to the floor. Slamming the door violently behind him, he turns so that his back is against it, and I am trapped. He slowly takes a long drag from his cigarette, then blows the smoke right in my face. "*You. Whore.*"

Then

I HAVE AN INTERESTING and extensive dating history for a girl my age. That's putting it nicely. I was a slut, a hoochie, a harlot. I knew it, and at the time, I liked it. The sex at least made me feel wanted. I was proud that I had the ability—dare I say power—to seduce whomever I wanted. That gave me a sense of having some kind of control over the opposite sex in at least one small area of my life. I've always had boyfriends, sometimes several casual relationships at a time. Because I could. I'm not saying it was right. I'm just telling the truth.

Early in my dating life, some boys were very normal: kind and sweet and not messed up like me. They were good guys, but once one boy had broken my trust, that was that, and I lumped all males together as liars. I was only thirteen when I really started dating and screwing around, so I should not have been shocked at the fact that these guys weren't perfect.

Nor should I have been shocked that they were not falling in love in about thirty seconds like I was with them. I was a kid and I was traumatized. They were still really just boys. And as they say, boys will be boys.

Somehow, by the age of fourteen, I had started dating older men, adults. I really don't remember how that happened. I made a conscious choice to hang around with a different crowd, an older crowd. These were not kids I knew from school. They were high school dropouts, the occasional college student, or people who had already graduated and were working. Some were just perverted bums, and I was so naïve, wild, and in a desperate search for love that I couldn't see that.

The first man I really became crazy over was when I was a not-so-sweet sixteen. I was already somewhat experienced, shall we say, with men by this point, but I was hooked on Peter instantly. After just two weeks of dating, Peter had me wrapped around his little finger, sweet-talking me into moving into a cheap and very tiny one-room apartment with him. Of course, I was thrilled! I finally found the love I had been looking for and a place to call home. I didn't care what home looked like. I cared what it felt like. I was ecstatic! I was finally wanted.

The apartment, or should I say, the bedroom, had olive-green shag carpet. It was in the basement of an old house, and the entrance was around back. We shared the small and dimly lit olive-green kitchen, bath, and living room with the other renters. That was creepy because they were all single, at least forty-something-year-old men. They seemed to only appear in the shared areas one at a time when Peter was gone, inviting me to smoke a cigarette or share a glass of scotch and water. Super sketchy and no thank you. My skin crawled around them. So when Peter was away, which was almost all the time, I just stayed in the bedroom, a prisoner of love, with the door locked. I did nothing for hours until Peter came home. That's how desperate I was to be loved.

Yes, we were super poor and had basically nothing. We definitely couldn't afford a TV, so I would just sit on the bed and daydream in this musty room with only a bed and a lamp in it about my future with Peter … for hours … and hours. I didn't even have a magazine or book to pass the time. Anyway, I still adored our place because of the simple fact that we shared it. I figured we could brighten up the drabness with our love and some bargain store décor when we could afford it.

Peter constantly swore his undying devotion to me, and I ate up every word. I totally believed in and trusted him. With Peter, I had many overwhelmingly positive feelings that I had never felt before. He said so many kind things to me. I couldn't get enough of it. Also, to be noted and not taken lightly, the sex with him was the first positive experience of sex I had ever had. And let's be honest, girls, sex, dare I say *most* sex, *especially* sex when you are young or not very experienced is not *good* sex. (You all *know* I'm telling the truth!)

I was head over heels. He was someone more mature. He had a different circle of friends, and I loved meeting new people. He was a man, not a boy, whom I was sure would protect me and provide for me. We didn't have much, but he had provided me with what I considered to be a loving home. Yes. My standards were very low. So, so low. But I took what little provision he offered as definitive proof of his devotion.

As much worldly experience as I already had, which was a lot for my age, I was still very naïve. I thought we had started to create the loving family and home that I had been longing for. Our small (and did I mention un-airconditioned?) apartment felt like a wonderful dream. I was safe in our tiny home (room) and madly in love. I thought Peter was *it* for me. Whatever came our way, we would face it together. Oh, the bliss of young love! I was in la-la land.

Fast-forward six days after I moved in with him. Yes. I said *six days*. Peter never came home from work. I was beside myself. Something *must* have happened to him! We didn't have a landline, so I just waited in our tiny bedroom crying. For days. I waited, worried, and sobbed. I didn't have any of his friend's phone numbers or addresses to even attempt to track him down. I kept hoping that he would show up or at least that one of his friends would swing by and tell me where he was. I waited and cried. Then I waited and cried some more. I was so confused and heartbroken. I felt sick. My stomach was in knots. I couldn't eat. I couldn't sleep. I jumped up, looking for him at every faint noise, thinking for sure he was coming back home. But it never was. It was always only one of the creepy old men who shared the house. My hopes would soar and then be dashed yet again.

I finally decided to go searching for Peter on foot. I didn't own a car, and Peter had taken his old Buick when he left. I walked all over town in the one-hundred-degree heat, trying to find him, but he was nowhere to be found. I had no idea where he could even be. It also occurred to me that I didn't really know much about him. I didn't know where he hung out. I didn't know who his best friend was. After several days of searching, coming up empty-handed, and crying myself to sleep, I got a tip from a friend as to where Peter might be found. Someone had seen his car parked down by one of the lakes on the outskirts of town. I walked and walked and walked as fast as I could to get there. I even tried hitchhiking to get across town, but no one picked me up. It took me at least a couple of hours.

I was a sweaty and exhausted wreck when I finally got there, but then, hope! There it was! Peter's Buick! I was thrilled and relieved until I realized that Peter was with another girl, hunched over her, naked, in the backseat of his car, doing *the deed* in broad daylight. His naked butt cheeks were up in the air for the world to see as he pumped away at her. I was completely shocked and heartbroken. After my exhilaration at the sight of his car, my emotions plummeted like you get riding a roller coaster, my heart dropping to my stomach in an instant when my mind grasped what was happening. It was unfathomable that any person would profess their undying love and devotion if it wasn't true. In six short days, I was garbage to him, unloved and unwanted. Again. *And* I had been replaced by this stranger. This *slut*! I had changed my entire pitiful life to be with him. I had big dreams, and he ripped them away without another thought.

Why? I kept asking myself over and over. I. Was. Devastated. Crushed. Inconsolable. And I was pissed off. I also had nowhere to go, which is how I became homeless. As if I needed things to get worse. This was my very first lesson in true disloyalty and in how the grown-up world can be very disappointing. This felt like experiencing the death of a loved one. I would never get him back or see him again.

I was drowning in misery and grief, but that didn't really matter because I had no one to comfort me. I felt completely hollow and utterly invisible.

After my initial shock and sadness, I got mad—furious, actually. My love turned into rage. And my rage turned into a plan for revenge. So I decided two could play his game, and I would beat him. We lived in a small town of just a few hundred people, and our social circles sometimes mingled with each other as they do in towns of that size. I vaguely knew who his friends were although I did not know them. I decided that since he didn't want me, he sure as heck would still see me looking my best and hear about all (and who) I was doing. He would never be able to get me back, but my plan was that he would eventually want to. I would not become invisible to him. I would date (screw) *all* his friends and anyone I thought he might possibly know. *He* would be the one missing out, and *I* would be the one having all the fun. This was how and why I became the girl with the reputation of being the best lay in town. I was making myself lovable. Very, very lovable. The reality was, I had to find someone new to screw really quickly so that I would have a place to stay.

I wandered around aimlessly for a few days, sleeping wherever I found a safe spot. Maybe it would be under a low-hanging tree or in an unlocked car in a parking lot until I randomly ran into one of Peter's buddies. He had already heard about the break-up. He had also heard that I was good in the sack. So like any kind-hearted, young, horny fella would do, he invited me to stay in his house. Of course, I said yes. It was thrilling to be in a house again, even if it was a drug house in the hood, full of people partying, slugs in the bathtub (for real), and no electricity. It was at least a roof over my head. I'm no dummy, so I took it. Of course, that meant that I slept in his bed. When the other girls who were also staying there weren't, that is. I was, after all, good old Lovable Luca. I was in survival mode. And his wish was my command.

Now

BACK IN JACK'S office, I am shocked into silence by his violent reaction. I had imagined his response would be excitement, happiness even. Up until this exact moment, I had been hoping for a quick marriage proposal, maybe even a spur-of-the-moment wedding so that we could become an official family. But here Jack stands, eyes blazing, calling me a worthless whore. He's screaming at me over the blaring of heavy metal music that wafts from the party through the sturdy office door as he roughly runs his fingers, agitated, through his hair. His mood shifts between silent fury and explosive.

He's threatening me, screaming. He's letting me know what a "piece of shit" I am. He's been pacing around the room like a caged animal as he screams. The next thing I know, Jack is over in the corner of the room and has opened up the wood and etched-glass gun cabinet. I hadn't actually noticed it until this moment. I watch, like this is a movie, as he pulls out a shotgun and checks to see that it is loaded. My mind does not register this at first. Then it does. Time seems to slow down. What is happening?

Jack is pointing the gun right at my head. Pushing the barrel in my face. "*You whore*! You *will* stay here all night! I'm calling the clinic first thing in the morning. I *will* be taking you to get an abortion! If you try to leave, I *will* kill you!" There is no debating him. No room for talking on my end. I just stand there, shocked into silence. He takes the shotgun with him as he storms out of the office, slamming the door shut, the walls reverberating with the force. My brain is whirling. My emotions are, at the same time, numb and spinning out of control. *What is going on?* I cannot grasp all that has just occurred in the span of about ten minutes.

Guns N' Roses "Welcome to the Jungle" is blaring from behind the door, and I think, *How fitting.* My next thought is that maybe someone from the party will come back here and check on me eventually. Then they could possibly help me. If someone talks to Jack and distracts him, maybe I can get away. Frantically, I scan for an exit. Maybe there is a way out of this room. But looking around, I quickly realize that, of course, there's not. There are a couple windows, but they are the skinny horizontal kind at the very top of the wall. Not the kind that open up or that a body, not even my small one, will fit through even if I smashed the glass out. Maybe Jack will get drunk and pass out, I hope. Then I could sneak past him and get outside to my car. Time feels like it is standing still, but it is passing and in darkness, nonetheless.

I'm scared and in a state of unbelief. Everything seems like a terrible dream. My brain is fuzzy. I was sure I had found real love this time. I'm in shock, but my emotions are fried. I feel like a robot. It was already late when I got here; it must be one a.m. by now. My mind will not stop reeling. I feel like I'm on a tilt-o-whirl, and my brain is trying to figure out how to stop the ride so I can climb off. *How am I going to get out of this? What's going to happen in the morning? Will I be alive? Will he really shoot me if I try to run for it? What's happening out there at the party? Do people know I'm here, being held against my will? If so, what has he told them? What can I do to get out of this? And … what about the baby?*

Then

IN ALL OF my partying, no matter how I played it, my underlying motive was only to find love. I was rough around the edges, but I just wanted to be seen, heard, and appreciated. Because I have always felt abandoned and alone, I craved being the most wanted, popular girl anywhere I went, and most of the time, I was. But I didn't just want to be popular, I also wanted to be actually cared for, protected, embraced, and cherished. I definitely had never experienced any of those things. I did what it took to get noticed and stand out when I felt it was necessary, but I could also blend into a crowd and get along with any sort of person with ease. I was a chameleon dressed in ever-changing short shorts and crop tops.

I tanned every morning at Life's a Beach, the small, two-bed salon in town, making my skin a buttery golden color year-round. I didn't eat for days at a time so that I would be the skinniest girl wherever I went. It felt so good to be skinny. People always mention it, how thin I looked and how I was tinier than everyone else. It's good for the self-esteem. You've gotta remember, this was the 1980s, a time when super models were extremely thin and very tan. (Think Elle Macpherson and Christie Brinkley.) I was aiming for their look, with the exception of my dark hair, of course, and I'd say I pretty much nailed it. I mean, I wasn't supermodel hot, but I *was* hotter than average. That still didn't seem to help make me more lovable.

As you know, I attempted to enjoy life. I got drunk. And I sometimes smoked some weed to chill out. I snuck out, had sex, went dancing, and drank at bars. I partied in the cornfields down by the river in our little Missouri town til all hours of the morning. I partied in the back seats of cars and city parks long after they were closed for the night. I willingly participated in most, if not all, of the sins they preached about at the small Baptist church where I grew up. Dad would have cringed if he knew everything I was up to. Jan couldn't have cared less, and of course, Mom was long gone. I've actually have not heard from her since the day she drove away. I added all these things to the never-ending list growing in my head of reasons I was unworthy of love. I mean, seriously. Whose parents don't even want them? I had nothing to lose, so I just kept trying harder and harder to prove that I deserved love. If I was just given the right chance, I knew I'd become lovable. Lovable Luca.

My silky black hair and sultry green eyes were show-stopping, and I knew it. Add these to the fact that I knew how to dance and flaunt my body, and when nighttime fell, I was a vixen, irresistible to men. I flirted with anyone I thought was cute or who I thought could provide something for me that would equal having a good time and at least the temporary feeling of being cared about. Don't get me wrong, I would do things for other people too. I wasn't selfish. I was surviving, and survival is a daily chess match with lots of give and take. I made a lot of calculated moves. I knew if I played things the right way that I could get lots of free stuff from different types of people. I got free booze, free weed, and other drugs. I could get free rides to parties, free motel rooms across the river to party in, and bags of free burgers at the local drive in. I could sweet talk gas or cigarette money out of a turnip. Anything I received, I was always willing to share with my friends.

If I was in just the right mood, I might even randomly offer a person sex, sometimes, even if I had just met them. I didn't mind sharing myself, as long as I liked a person. It wasn't like I was worth much anyway, and sex made me feel wanted. I thought that maybe sex with the right person, no matter how it started, could lead to love. You don't know unless you try, right?

My mind and heart were traumatized. I had been told for so long and for so often that I was worth nothing, most parts of me believed it. I was trying to show anyone who would hang around long enough that I was a person of value. I was always trying to prove that I mattered. I was also looking for validation that I wasn't invisible. *Look how cute I am! Look how funny I am! Look what I will do for you! I am lovable, and I will prove it!* So if I was being noticed, I definitely was not invisible. (Feeling invisible sucks, by the way.) Almost everyone who met me loved me. I had scads of friends, but I felt lost.

The party life was like a Ferris wheel. Up for a few minutes, having a blast and then down the next because, of course, everything was fun, until the booze ran out, the sun came up, and the guy I had been making out with disappeared into the sunrise, never to be heard from again. Morning left me suddenly praying like a backslider at a tent revival that whoever I had screwed didn't have gonorrhea—or something even worse. I left most parties feeling bone-tired, dirty, and totally unworthy of the love I was trying to find. Deep down, I was ashamed of the things I did. Daylight just made me feel even more filthy and unlovable.

Now

MY ADRENALINE IS wearing off. I've paced Jack's office over and over and over and over. I've tried to create a plan to get out. I've panicked and calmed myself more than a few times. I have no idea what time it is, but several hours must've passed since Jack threatened to kill me. There's no clock, but it's still dark outside. I look around for, what, I don't know. I tiptoe to the wooden door and crack it open. I peer through the sliver down the dark hall into the living room. It feels miles away although it's just a few yards. I'm totally isolated. I feel like a mouse in a cage with a mad scientist watching. Like I'm trapped in one of those mazes where, at the end, there is only death. Music is still blasting. I don't know how much more Skid Row, Iron Maiden, and Motley Cru I can take. People are still hanging out in the living room, but judging by the volume of the voices, the crowd seems to be slowly leaving, and the party's winding down. Not a soul has come to check on me. I'm sure I'm forgotten by everyone here by now. Except Jack.

I'm getting tired, and I have to pee. I sit down on the only chair in the room. It's ripped-up, faded, fake black leather, the type that rolls up to a desk. I fidget. I stand back up. I stretch. I sit back down. I try to roll around in the chair, but the wheels don't move very well on the old, stained carpet. I sit still. I kick my foot off the floor and make the seat spin in circles. I pick at a hangnail on my thumb. I listen for any sound of Jack approaching, but there is none. I sigh. I start to panic again and force myself to slow my breathing. I chew on my bottom lip. It's dry. I'm really thirsty, and I still have to pee. I'm very uncomfortable, but this chair is all there is to sit on. I lean back, tilting my face to the ceiling. I close my eyes and do nothing but think. I decide to just keep my eyes closed. I'm exhausted.

As I'm resting my eyes, a thought runs through my mind out of nowhere. *Maybe I should pray. No. Way.* I push it down. *My life is a mess, and it is all because of my sin! Sin! Sin! Sinner! Whore! Idiot! Sinner! God can't hear you, you worthless, dirty, unlovable slut!!* The hateful words roar inside my head. I am terrified. Oddly, I am not heartbroken at Jack's betrayal. Suddenly I couldn't care less about him. It's like he is emotionally dead to me. My mind is only on the baby. What will happen when daylight comes? How can I get away? How can I get out of this? When is Jack coming back? Will he still have the gun? Morning will be here soon.

Then

WELL, AFTER MORE than a few disappointing boyfriends, I decided to clean up my act. Around age sixteen, I started to think that maybe my heart and soul would feel better if I did some things differently. I was getting nowhere acting totally feral, plus I would be turning seventeen soon. That's the age I could legally get into a lot more trouble for some of the stuff I was doing. I was trying to find love, not go to jail. My inward turmoil sometimes turned into outward aggression. I would fight anyone over anything if I felt disrespected. I got arrested sometimes, and I won't lie, I feel powerful when I won a fight. Making people feel scared of me created the illusion that I had some type of power. If others feared me, I felt looked up to and respected. Creating fear in others gave me the illusion that I was somewhat in control.

I hopped between groups of people that didn't even like each other (but they all liked me) to try to find what I was missing. The people within this older, rough crowd were not loving or the type to settle down. They were the "we're gonna end up in prison and we don't care" type. I don't know how, but I just knew that I had to change who I hung out with and how I was acting to get different results because what I was doing wasn't working. At all. My goal was still simply to find unconditional love. And I wasn't finding it.

Like I said, I was raised in church. And when I started acting up as tweenager, I completely stopped going. There were a ton of services, in case you don't know this: Sunday morning, Sunday night, and Wednesday night services, plus other activities like Sunday school, choir practice, Bible study, camp, handbell practice, potlucks, etc. I got tired of feeling judged at all of it. I still had one friend from church who attended faithfully. Stacy always invited me to "come back anytime" when she saw me at the Piggly Wiggly or the feed store. Her continual caring, nonjudgemental attitude, and friendliness spoke to something deep in my soul. I felt like she was a true believer in Christ because she actually acted like a goodhearted Christian and was a generally kind person. She lived like she talked, which was rare. Because of her, I decided one random Sunday to give going to church another whirl.

I just thought, if there was one good Christian person on earth, there must be more somewhere. This time, I tried a different church than the one that had been so unwelcoming a few years before. And what do you know? It was all right. That same day, I got right with the Lord. Again. I swore to myself and Jesus, in tears up at the altar as the choir sang "Amazing Grace," that I would do better.

Keeping good on my promise, I switched my life up and started hanging around kids my age that were still in school. I started doing the normal things that kids in my grade were actually supposed to do. We went to school dances and football games and hung out at each other's houses, watching TV, not misbehaving. I had also almost totally stopped drinking. That was a big deal because before this, when I got my paycheck, the first thing I'd do after I cashed my check on Friday at the bank was go buy a handle of Jim Beam. Just for me. Buying and drinking a bottle of bourbon was always easy for me. I got wasted on weekends regularly. I mean, like black-out drunk. Looking back, it's a miracle that I didn't die of alcohol poisoning or drunk driving or some other horrific accident.

Now, I had cut way back on the booze. I went from guzzling a bottle of hard liquor every Friday to sipping an occasional beer. I had stopped smoking the devil's lettuce too. And call the press! I stopped screwing everyone on God's green earth. That was the biggest change. I did still have my cigarettes though. So I chain-smoked, loved Jesus, and had only one boyfriend who was very kind. He never pushed having sex on me, and I really liked him a lot. We had lots of good, clean fun, like going dancing at the honky-tonk on Saturday nights. I thought I was falling in love. Real love. We were actually friends, and I was trying to be a better person for myself, for him, and for those around me. Life was going pretty well, and I actually felt happy for once.

Now

I MUST HAVE DOZED off. I startle awake to absolute silence. The party is definitely over. The sun is shining through those two tiny, hateful little windows that my body can't squeeze out of. My neck is stiff, and I have to pee so bad, I can hardly hold it because I never got to go last night. I was too scared to try to even open the door all the way for fear of getting shot. Slowly, I rub my stiff neck and stand. I stay really still, listening. I hold my breath and wait. I don't hear a thing. I decide to take a chance and slowly crack open the office door. Its hinges let out a slow, low, loud groan. Damn! I pause for a second, my body going cold with fear. But my bladder cannot wait. I step one foot out into the hallway, and suddenly, Jack is there, blocking my way with an icy stare.

I try my best to be nonchalant and act like last night did not happen. I'm just here, you know, casually trying to stay alive. I cautiously make eye contact and try to gauge his mood. He does not look furious anymore, and I don't see the shotgun. "I have to pee." I cross my legs as I stand there trying to hold it in.

"Good," he responds gruffly. "I already called the clinic, and they need your first piss of the morning for the pregnancy test. I'm taking you to get an abortion now. Go get in the car." I. Am. Stunned. All thought escapes my mind. Any hope I have left drains from my soul. A million words jumble in my head but I cannot speak. Jack shifts his body slightly so that I can get down the hallway, but he blocks the bathroom door. He's refusing to let me pee here at his house. My mind races. What do I do? What do I do? *What do I do*? Tears well up in my eyes, and I blink and move rapidly away from the bathroom I never get to use, trying my hardest not to let the tears fall. I'm also trying not to wet my pants. I really don't think I can hold it much longer. I'm trying not to let him know that I know he has the upper hand. I'm trying to act like I can hold it *another* eight hours. I feel like either my bladder is going to burst, or I'm just going to pee my pants. But I'm in the living room now, and Jack has followed very closely behind me. *Keep your game face on*, I think. *Just breathe.*

I turn to try to think of something to say to him. Something that will get me out of here safely, but I can't think of anything. My mind goes blank. All of a sudden, it's like my body has even forgotten (again) that I needed to pee. I don't know if that's some kind of survival mechanism or what. Outside, it's early autumn and it's chilly. Jack grabs his ratty blue-jean jacket with its faded plaid lining and shrugs it on. I don't have a jacket, and he does not offer me one. Jack obviously couldn't care less.

Making eye contact with me, he picks up a silver revolver from the top of his stereo cabinet and places it casually into his jacket's inner pocket. "If you try to leave, I will kill you. If you run, I will kill you. If you come out of the clinic still pregnant, I will kill you. Let's go." I know he means business. I. Am. Terrified. Not seeing any other options, I walk outside with him, a prisoner of his insanity, and we both get into his car. To the casual observer, all is well, but it is not. I buckle up. You know, for my safety. Haha.

Then

AS IT TURNS out, sometimes trying to be better doesn't work out as planned. I did really well for a while. I was going to church, and I had high hopes for my life and for my relationship with my newest boyfriend. We'd been together for several months, and we even hung out sometimes with his family. That was a huge deal to me. I liked them all, and I was falling in love. I was terrified to tell him this because what if he didn't feel the same way? I didn't think I could stand it if he rejected me. I knew that teen couples broke up all the time even solid ones who had been together way longer than us. I was also scared of any intimacy with him. I was already head over heels, and I was a little afraid that by not doing anything sexual, I would lose him. I kept telling myself that I did not need to worry about that because he was truly a kind guy. A good one. I was also trying to be a good Christian, and so I was trying not to act like a slut with him. As it turns out, apparently when a teenage boy dates a teenage girl that is known to put out after a few dates, and that boy is not getting anything but kisses and an occasional hand job, he usually starts to wonder why she isn't putting out *for him*. My brilliant teenage mind never thought of the fact that he would *want to* and probably thought he definitely *would* have sex with me.

Just because I was trying to do better morally didn't mean that he didn't want to have sex with me. I imagined that when we finally did have sex and I *did* want to, it would be us, as an actual couple, making love. "Making love" was something I did not normally do. I only fucked. By mentally telling myself it was "just a fuck," I put most of my emotions on a distant shelf somewhere and left them out of the situation. That way, I was sure not to get hurt again. My boyfriend and I discussed none of this, however. I just assumed things between us would stay amazing and would go the way they were outlined in my head. Everything was great, and I thought it would keep getting better. My mistake.

I was very bad at communicating my feelings because I was so terrified of being told I wasn't wanted and then getting hurt again. I was so used to being told I wasn't enough that I did not want to ever risk hearing that from him. So I said nothing about my growing feelings or about why I wasn't having sex with him. We spent all our time together, and I was enjoying our wholesome fun. We only made out for a few minutes, but we did that quite often, so, looking back, he must have had blue balls the size of Texas grapefruits that he never mentioned to me. I think you see where this is heading. But I was oblivious.

You can imagine my surprise, when one Monday at school, I heard a rumor that he had thrown a party the prior weekend. I was totally unaware of this party and thought it couldn't be true. I, of all people, would know if my very steady boyfriend had a party. And I would be the number one person there. Of course. The weekend in question had been the first weekend we had ever been apart during our relationship. He had told me some very normal reason that I can't recall now as to why we couldn't hang out the previous Friday. Something like he had to babysit his younger siblings. And I had believed him. I had no reason not to. I thought he was my best friend.

A few minutes later, at school, I heard another rumor: that he had had sex with a girl at the party. *What*? I'd been a little bothered by the first rumors, but now I was getting pissed and more than a little worried. I still didn't really believe what I was hearing, though. No way were the stories true! Everyone had to be lying!

Oddly, it was very hard for me to find him that day. He seemed to be missing from all our usual spots, and I knew he was at school. His truck was in the parking lot. I finally caught up to him, purely by accident, in the cafeteria. When I asked him about the rumors, praying they were false, I was devastated to learn the truth. He told me point blank that he had, in fact, had a party, did not invite me, and had sex with a random girl. He didn't seem bothered that I became upset at all. He just stared blankly at me until I tearfully ran off. And that was that. We broke up right then and there. My heart was broken.

My attempt to be good had not worked and had actually backfired. I had not found the love I was hoping for, and this felt much worse than just screwing around because I had started taking my walls down for this guy. Our relationship had given me hope, friendship, and respect. Until it didn't. I had once again been dreaming of a future that was not going to become reality. My days of being good were over. Being good, acting better, and trying to hold on to morals had failed me. I felt that God had failed me too. I had been praying, having faith, and starting to hope. And then hope had crushed me when I least expected it.

My stomach felt like it was full of rocks. I ran to the bathroom and actually threw up. Then I put back up every invisible wall I had built around my heart before and then added some extras, just in case. I bolted from school and straight back to my old, no-good buddies. I needed to have a mind-numbingly good time. I needed a buzz. I needed to drown my sorrows. Break out that whiskey, baby. Bad Luca was back, and she needed a stiff drink.

Now

THE DRIVE TO the clinic is tense. My mind whirls. *Surely, a person can't just show up and get an abortion?* I know nothing about this. I mean, the clinic people didn't even talk to me on the phone. *Did Jack really call them this morning?* I think he did. He seems to know some things, like them apparently needing my pee. He also seems to know a price. The only thing he says to me the entire ride is, "Don't worry, I have the cash." (That is *not* what I'm worried about. I'm worried about getting away!) He's sitting there in the driver's seat like he doesn't have a care in the world, smoking nonchalantly and asking me if I want a cigarette. Like this whole scene isn't absolutely nuts.

I flatly respond, "No." I think, *Where did all this go wrong*? Can I try to make a deal with God? You don't grow up in church and *not* think of God at a time like this. That just doesn't happen. I want the baby. I also want to stay alive.

I don't know how to get out of this, but obviously, Jack is a psycho. How did I not see any signs of this before now? Should I jump out of the car? Can I run when we get there? Maybe they will help me. Maybe there will be an emergency exit there, in the clinic, but away from him.

Jack is devoid of all emotion. He is driving like this is a taxi and I am his fare. The tires crunching down the gravel road remind me of tiny skeletons being crushed and snapping apart. Well, that's morbid. And fitting. Where did that thought come from? I just breathe. In and out. In and out. I don't move. I don't make a sound. Bile rises in my throat. I swallow it back down.

I stare blankly out the window. I grew up here, but I'm in an almost trance-like state, and I don't know where we are. I should, but I just don't. My mind cannot handle one more thing. Everything is a blur. I feel so heavy. Tired. Exhausted. The adrenaline has worn off yet again, and I feel invisible in the world. I'm totally insignificant. Smaller than an ant. A dirty, worthless nobody. How could I have let this happen? By the sound of the tires, Jack has turned off the gravel and onto a paved road. I am just too overcome by trauma and stress to comprehend where we are. Even in the daylight. My mind snaps to attention. We're driving on pavement, which means we are in the next town over. That's where the clinic is.

I try to focus. We're getting close. My heart pitter-patters. I slowly recall that I still have to pee. I look up, and we are here. At the clinic. Jack parks. I think I'm going to throw up. I will myself not to. Jack turns to me and says brightly, "We're here, sugar." Sugar. That's what he always calls me when he's being loving. It's his little pet name for me, and I have always loved it until this very second. Because he just used this name, I feel an inkling of hope until I look into his eyes. They are reptilian. Cold, empty, and dangerous.

"Get out of the car," he quietly and sternly orders, patting his jacket pocket. I slowly unbuckle my seatbelt and obey. I feel myself slipping into what I can best describe as dissociation. We walk into the clinic together. I feel numb and robot-like. A receptionist not much older than me asks how she can help us. Jack speaks nonchalantly to her. I stand mute and unmoving at Jack's side. They exchange words, but I can't focus. I can't grasp what is being said. My mind is a jumbled mess. *Please, please, please, please, please* keeps running non-stop through my head like some kind of silent mantra. Jack hands the lady a wad of cash. She hands me a cup for a urine sample.

They need my urine. That much I understand. The bathroom door is right next to the receptionist desk. Not knowing what else to do, I go pee. But I don't feel the relief you'd expect after all these hours of holding it. Jack stands on guard right outside the door. My hands visibly shake when I hand the full cup in its little biohazard bag back to the lady. Surely she will notice my nervous tremors. Will she look up and make eye contact with me? Maybe then I can signal her. She does not. It's obvious now that she will be no help. I'm just another number. By the time I sit down, my trembling has turned more violent. She doesn't seem to notice or care. Jack sits right next to me and grips my thigh tightly. So. Tightly. It's his reminder to me. His wordless warning. As if I'd somehow forget that he has a gun in his jacket. As if I've already disregarded his threats. A sense of dread overwhelms me.

And we wait.

Then

I WAS BAD LUCA. I stopped going to church (again) and started screwing lots of guys (also again). I drank a lot, even more than I used to, to drown out the hurt. I was older now and a little wiser. I really thought I had something good going in that last relationship, but it just ended up breaking my heart even more. Trusting people was no longer an option. Playing them for survival was. *Sorry God, I just don't think the love I'm looking for is out there. I am disappointed in myself and disgusted with everyone else. That includes you, God. I was sure you were going to help me out. And I tried my best. I really tried to be better. I* was *better. I tried to be responsible. I tried to be a good Christian. And I still got screwed over. Again. I was responsible with everything. I showed up for work and did a great job. I paid my bills. I went to church. I filed my taxes. I don't lie. I don't cheat. I'm trying not to cuss. I wasn't having sex. I wasn't getting drunk. I wasn't fighting people. I was trying so hard.*

But when I got screwed over this time, I totally stopped being responsible with myself, my body, and my life. I no longer cared about myself at all. I was not suicidal. I just did whatever came around, and I thought that if I happened to die having fun, oh well. Who cared? Because if I wasn't worth anything, then anything was worth doing. As we all know by now, I didn't matter to anyone, and I was definitely unlovable. So it didn't really matter if I continued to exist. My life was a gamble. Let the cards fall where they may. I was going to be out there, having a good time, self-medicating my broken heart even if all I really still want is to be Lovable Luca.

Now

WHAT? SITTING IN the clinic, Jacks vice-like grip suddenly releases from my thigh. Is someone talking? A garbled voice like the teacher from the *Peanuts* cartoon is saying something. I am totally zoned out here in the chilly waiting area of the clinic. Jack nudges me with his elbow, hard in the ribs, and hatefully whispers, "They called you. GO." I don't look at him. I don't look up. I don't blink. I don't do anything except stand up mechanically and proceed as ordered. I follow some definitely too-cheerful staff girl into a dimly lit room that holds only a small desk and two metal folding chairs. She smiles at me as she motions at me to sit down as if this were not where they murder babies. (I have always been pro-life. How ironic). She shuts the door, quickly handing me a pen and flipping through a thin stack of papers. "Sign here for the procedure." I keep my eyes and head down. I sign. She does not ask me anything. She does not ask, "Do you want this? Has anyone forced you here? Are you ok? Are you sure?" Nothing.

In their ads, this place says they offer counseling before all this. I've heard them. A lot. Counseling, my ass. I am completely terrified and speechless. I look up at her. She is looking at the paperwork. I try to open my mouth to speak up. My mouth is parched. My heart races. I picture Jack, blowing my head off with one shot. My mouth becomes drier than it already is. I keep it shut. I lick my lips. I feel like I've swallowed a brick. I feel like I'm being dragged ever so slowly beneath a menacing current that wants to swallow me whole.

I try to speak again. "Umm…"

"Yes?"

I mentally picture the gun in Jack's pocket. I imagine that I start to run. Right out of this awful clinic, through the lobby, past Jack, and right out the front door. Down the busy street, I run as hard and fast as I can while he chases me. I can't turn to look, but he is pulling the pistol from his pocket. His footsteps pound on the pavement, and he's gaining on me. Gaining on me. Gaining on me. He should be aiming the gun at me any minute, but I just keep running. *Blast*! I jerk in my seat. "Nothing. Never mind." I whisper in a voice that sounds so tiny and childlike, it's not at all like my own.

My ears are buzzing like an out-of-body experience. Someone else seems to be following all these commands, moving my body for me. As I am sitting there, stunned at myself for signing the paper, the door opens and in walks another lady. She says simply, "Come with me." Then, she stands there staring at me, unsmiling, unblinking. I stand up. And shiver. Not because I'm cold. Because I'm scared shitless.

I'm silently led to a dressing room and am quickly shown how to put on a hospital gown. I'm told to step through a door to the patients-only waiting area after I'm dressed in the gown.

I'm completely overwhelmed and still numbly glancing around with each step I take, looking for an escape, a glowing red exit sign, anything to run to, so that maybe I can sneak out the back and get away, half-naked in my gown and all. My furtive glances don't find an exit.

As I step into the dimly lit patient-waiting area, my mind once again becomes more in touch with the reality of what is happening. In this large, open room, there is a circle of recliners, filled with girls like me in gowns. We all face each other silently. Expressionless. It is super weird. I was not expecting to see other girls. There is no small talk. The air is thick with tension and heaviness. Everyone sort of glances at each other and then quickly looks away if eye contact is even made. Each person is sitting in their recliner, staring at the floor. *What the hell? Why am I in a room full of strangers? This is fucked up.* I don't usually use that word anymore, but I'm sorry, it's fitting for this situation. I look for an exit. Again. And I still don't see any way out. There are a few unmarked, metal, closed doors, but none that appear to lead outside.

We sit together but very separate in our silent circle like a newly formed Girl Scout troop waiting for an abortion activity badge on our sashes. It is ominously silent. I have never in my life been in a room full of so many girls that was this silent. It feels like a tomb, hushed, eerie, and tragic. One by one, each girl is called, like a precious lamb being led to slaughter. I have no idea if it has been ten minutes or thirty when each reappears. The place is set up so that you can't really keep track of time even if you wanted to. One by one, a person in scrubs leads each girl quickly back to their same recliners. The person then vanishes. As each girl enters and sits back down, a female attendant appears at their side seemingly out of nowhere. This server encourages her to "drink some juice and eat a cookie" from the tray she is holding out. After each girl takes her drink and snack, she is told lightly, "When you feel ready, you may get dressed and go."

My mind is going berserk. It is tweaking out. Time glitches by in my mind in fragmented pieces. I zone out, then my mind snaps back to reality after I don't know how long. Yes, this is real, but it feels like a movie broken into scenes. I am numb. I am powerless. I am panicked like a deer in headlights. I am frozen. I want to run but I can't. I see terrible things coming, but my brain cannot think of how to avoid what happens next. In one second, I'm simultaneously praying, thinking of baby names, wondering if it's a boy or a girl, and looking for an exit. I'm wondering, *If I run, will Jack see me? Where is he? Would he catch me? How far does his gun shoot? How fast can I run? What am I supposed to do? I want my baby! Someone, please notice that something is not right*! My brain screams silently. *I should just run, and if I get shot, I get shot. But which door is out?* I can't feel my body. I am breathing too fast. I'm covered in sweat. *Someone, help me*, I think.

"Luca." I look up and a nurse is standing next to me. It's my turn.

Then

BAD LUCA DID it again. The night started out fine, just the usual party. Lots of people. A keg. Some jungle juice. Blah, blah, blah. You know the drill. Boring when it's the same every weekend. I was ready for something different again. Something more personal. What I had been doing, once again, was not enough. I was tired of being lonely and had started to have the familiar feeling that I wanted to try to settle down once more. Games are only fun for so long because they are also so mentally exhausting. Well, there I was. Partying it up. Minding my own business and wondering where I would end up by morning. Then *he* walked in. Who was *this*? I had never seen this guy before and he was cute. He was older and not from my normal group of friends. I knew I liked him. I was instantly drawn to him. It was a magnetic attraction. *Sizzle.*

Within minutes, we had made eye contact across the room and were flirting away. A few moments after that, I knew his name was Jack, and he had already claimed me as his. He was holding my hand and calling me "sugar." I loved it! He was letting everyone know (already) that I was his. I felt wanted, protected, and like he was putting everyone there on notice. The unspoken message was, "This is my woman. She is off limits."

Yes! I'd finally found a man's man. One who would stand up for me. He kept his arm around me throughout the party, pulling me close. He also attended to my every need like a gentleman. I loved physical attention, and I loved people seeing that I was wanted, no, *taken*, by him. *Sorry, fellas in line. You can't have me. I'm taken by Jack.* My heart throbbed and swelled. I was so happy it hurt. I felt like I would burst. We hung out for hours and hours. At the end of the night, Jack was very polite. He was kissing me goodnight and softly whispering that he couldn't wait to see me again when I asked unashamedly, "So, you're not going to sleep with me?" He stopped talking and stopped kissing me, a look of surprise crossing his face. "Pretty please?" I asked, giving him an innocent but seductive smile as my emerald-green eyes melded deeply into his liquid brown ones. He couldn't resist my offer. He did indeed sleep with me, and we were an item from that night on and a serious couple immediately.

Being with Jack started feeling like home to me. It was true love. I was sure. Within months, every time we were together, Jack talked about marrying me. We had no concrete plans, but we daydreamed about it together often. I loved that. The promise of a future together was full of hope and fun. We never had any problems. There was never stress or anger between us. We just hung out, enjoying each other and everything was going wonderfully. Until my positive pregnancy test, that is. And until I walked into his party last night to share the news. And until he held me at gunpoint and forced me to go to the clinic where they get rid of unwanted "problems." Everything was great, until it wasn't. Until…

Now

AS I WALK back to my recliner from the procedure room, trembling and bleeding, I am overwhelmed with sadness. I feel empty and hollow. I no longer feel fear. I feel … odd. A little more broken. A bit more invisible. A lot more stupid. Much, much more unforgivable. I feel like a horrendous loser. This is not a mistake I can ever fix. What I've done is done. Forever. Eternally. A tangible heaviness weighs me down. A vast sadness swallows me as if I am getting sucked into quicksand. And here comes that damn lady with her cookies and juice. "I. Don't. Want. Any. Leave. Me. Alone. Go. Away." She blinks like a lizard. I stare her down. My eyes blaze with a look that says, "I dare you to say something else to me" until she walks away. I just sit and sit and sit. There is no undoing this. I feel awful physically, emotionally, and I guess I would say spiritually too. I have done the unthinkable. I feel like a baby killer. Because I am one. *I killed my baby, who up until last night, I was picking out a name for. I guess Jack is right. I. Am. A. Whore. An. Unforgiveable. Whore.*

Anger bubbles and swells up inside my chest out of nowhere. I feel a sudden and all-encompassing rage toward myself. I have somehow become what I do not even agree with. I did the unthinkable. *Oh. My. God. God? Are you here? Hey God. It's me. So obviously, you, um … know that I uhhh … shit. Sorry about the cussing, God. And I'm really sorry I just went through with* this. *Ummm … anyway, as You already know, I really fucked up this time. Sorry about the cussing (again), God. I don't think you can forgive this, but … I'm really, really, really, really, really, sorry. I didn't know what to do. I'm so sorry, God. I'm so, so, so, so, sorry.* My heart breaks even more than I knew it could during this desperate prayer that has suddenly developed in my head and heart.

I'm on the verge of sobbing. I get up slowly, deciding it's time to get out of here. With the movement, blood gushes between my legs. I will not cry in this room full of gowned strangers. I did not choose this. Or did I? Thus, the mind game of my lifetime begins. Right now. *Did I do all I could? Did I, God? Should I have run? Where would I have gone? Did I just wuss out? Am I just a wuss who is making excuses, God? I didn't even attempt to speak to get help before it was too late. I didn't just say no to the doctor or nurse.* All I know for sure is that now, I do not need to think of any baby names. My heart feels like it's crumpling in on itself. As if jagged little fragments of my soul are breaking off at a very rapid pace. One shard free-falls, then another, and another, and another. They plummet down. Down. Down. Each one lands right in the malevolent, condemning pit of hell. *I have to get out of here.*

I can't really remember getting dressed. I also can't remember walking into the lobby and finding Jack, still on armed-guard duty in the waiting area. But a mental snapshot of his face with his smile plastered on it is etched into my brain. A smirk comes alive in his eyes. He stands slowly, casually, from his chair as if he's not my captor in this building full of death. I am his forced accomplice to what I believe is murder. His eyes are now twinkling. *Twinkling*! He has a huge, happy, shit-eating grin and twinkly eyes. I want to punch him right in his hideous face. He was a very handsome guy to me until this. Now all I see is a hideous demon. Jack is absolute evil and disgusting. I am revolted to be in his presence. I am too weak and too broken to speak.

I will never forget his totally blissful and sickening ear-to-ear grin when he saw me walk out from the back of the clinic, pale and nauseated, no longer pregnant. He is a monster. *A monster*! This is the worst thing I have ever done. It is probably unforgivable. My mind screams again, "*You unforgiveable whore*!" My whole body is vibrating, trembling. I'm shivering and cannot stop.

I don't recall walking out of that awful clinic or how I got to be standing next to Jack's Camaro with the door opened. "Get in," Jack orders. He's already in with the motor running. "So, sugar, I'm having a party tonight if you want to come," he says nonchalantly as I gingerly climb into the passenger seat. *He. Is. So. Full. Of. Shit.* I'm disgusted. I don't speak. I can't. I don't wear a seatbelt because safety no longer matters. *I* no longer matter. I ride back to our little town in

Jack's car, feeling suffocated by rock music and nauseating cigarette smoke. I'm pretty sure I'm surrounded by a whole bunch of damnation in here too.

I have to ride with him back to his house because my car is still parked in the yard from last night. I don't want to go back. Not ever. But I have no choice. I need to get away from him. Now. I cannot believe what has happened in the last twenty-four hours. I'm living a horrendous dream. *How can this be happening?*

We ride and ride with his stupid heavy metal music blasting. He's chain-smoking those damn Marlboro Reds. The ashtray in the car is overflowing with crumpled cigarette butts. The smell makes me nauseated. I'm starting to have really bad cramps. I'm feeling physically worse by the minute. I'm a little dizzy and unbelievably thirsty. I breathe through each wave of cramps as I clench the door handle with a white-knuckled grip. I feel clammy, and I've started dripping with a cool sweat. I don't complain about it, and Jack pretends not to notice. I bow over in agony. I try to breathe through it. I inhale slowly through my nose and blow breath out through my mouth. I lean to the right, resting the side of my face against my window. It's hard to hold my head up. I need to lie down. Once we pull up to Jack's house, I silently and gingerly climb out of his car and get away from him as fast as I can. At this point, I'm moving pretty slowly as bad as I'm feeling.

Jack sits, watching with a smirk. My head spins. I grab onto my car so I don't fall as I slowly open the door to get in. I don't even glance Jack's way. I start the drive home. I hope I can make it. I don't feel well at all. And I never want to see Jack again.

Now: Continued

BY SOME SMALL miracle, I get home without passing out or throwing up. Luckily, it was not a very far drive from his place to mine. I feel woozy, and my stomach is in knots. I park and shakily make my way into the tiny rental home I share with my roommate, Marie, since I came home from college. She hears me shuffling down the hall toward my bedroom and peeks around the corner. Last she knew, I was happily pregnant. She was the only one who knew about it, and she has no idea what has occurred over the last twenty-four hours.

She sees me holding onto the wall for support and knows something is terribly wrong. As I get to my room and limply fall face down onto my bed in a pile of exhaustion and sadness, Marie is beside me and sitting next to me. I cannot speak. Tears are streaming down my face. I look up at Marie, and

I don't know where to even begin. Marie says, "Are you ok? You look pale."

I am shivering uncontrollably. I try several times to tell her what happened before I can actually utter a small portion of the horror that I have been through. When I do, she is speechless.

This is not how she nor I had thought any of this would go. When we last talked, it was about planning a baby shower. "Oh Luca!" she exclaims in a shocked whisper. Jumping up, she bends over and hugs me tightly. Grabbing a soft blanket, she covers me up, rubbing my back exactly as I imagine a loving mom would do. She darts around the house, semi-panicked, getting me some ice water, Kleenex, and ibuprofen, and asking what else I need. She offers to make me some food, but I cannot stomach that right now. I take a sip of water and flop my head back onto my feather pillow. It feels nice. With the fluffy blanket tucked around me, exhausted, I fall asleep.

When I wake, my pants are soaked with blood. I try to get up quickly, but the room spins with any movement. I sit and wait to gain my bearings, then I get up very slowly to go to the bathroom and clean myself up. I feel weaker than I did before, but I figure that's normal for what I've just been through. Marie hears me rustling around and rushes in. She has been to the local drugstore and brought me much needed supplies. She has a bag full of maxi pads, more ibuprofen, and even a heating pad. She has also brought me my favorite candy bar, Snickers. Seeing my blood-soaked pants on the bathroom floor, her jaw drops. "Is that much blood … normal?" she asks.

I have no idea. I shrug. "I guess." But to be honest, I am worried. I *really, really* do not feel well, and the bleeding is continuing at a steady flow. The amount is a lot more than my periods ever were, and they were always very heavy. I am becoming increasingly concerned. I have been home now for several hours. I thought the bleeding would be slowing down. I can't do anything about it, though, and I feel totally drained. So I just sit here half naked on the toilet, elbows on my thighs, head in my hands, too tired to move.

I finally get cleaned up with the help of Marie when she wanders in, worried, finding me still sitting on the toilet, slumped over. I should be at least slightly embarrassed as shy as I am, but I don't have the strength to wash up and get redressed all by myself. And I feel too bad to care.

This is taking way too much effort. I have to hold on to her, my arm around her waist, to make it the few steps from the bathroom back to my bed. I'm shivering again. Marie looks at me, worried, but doesn't say anything. I sit at the edge of the bed long enough to eat one bite of the candy bar and take a few swallows of water. I have to go to sleep. I'm so tired. I lay down, and I am out like a light for the rest of the day.

I wake up sometime in the middle of the night, freezing. My sheets feel wet. I reach down and gently pat them. Yes. My sheets are damp, and so am I. All over. The smell of copper gives it away. I know it's blood. I try to sit up and cannot. I'm far too weak. The room is dark. I try to call for Marie, but only a whisper escapes my parched lips. I have to get up and get to the bathroom. I try to sit up again. Nope. It's not happening. I lay there for a few minutes, trying to figure out what to do. My mind feels foggy. I decide to sort of twist onto my belly and slide out of bed. Here I go. Roll! Now I'm face first on my mattress. That tiny movement was much harder than I expected. I have to rest. I can't catch my breath. *Ok*, I think, *just slide your legs off the bed first and hold yourself up with your arms as you go.* Wham! My body hits the floor with a thud. It is not a soft landing.

I'm too lethargic to have any real control of my body. I lay there on the hard wood, face down, breathing heavily. I close my eyes. When I open them, I don't know how long it has been. Marie is shaking me, yelling my name. "Luca! Luca! Wake up!" I open my eyes. She has rolled me onto my back. The blinding light startles me. I blink. Blink. Blink. Blink. Everything is fuzzy. Where am I? Oh, yeah. The floor. I was on my way to the bathroom when I fell. "Oh, good," I whisper. "I need you to help me. I'm just going to the bathroom." I start to crawl on what is now a bloodied bedroom floor.

Marie is freaking out. "We have to call someone! I'm calling 911!" she urges.

"No!" I reply as loudly as I can muster. If we call an ambulance, Dad will find out. He cannot find out about this. This abortion. This *sin*. "No way are we calling anyone," I manage to get out. "No one can know." I am wracked with guilt. This is my worst sin by far. *You. Unforgiveable. Whore. You did this. Whatever happens, you brought it on yourself.* This runs through my jumbled mind as I make it to the bathroom by half crawling, half dragging myself there on my hands and knees. Grabbing the cool porcelain of the toilet, I pull myself up slowly. I pause to rest once I'm sitting on the tiled floor, resting my forehead on the edge of the cool seat. After a few minutes, I use the rest of my energy to climb to a seated position, pantless, onto the porcelain throne. My heart is beating so fast, and I am panting from the strain of moving. I'm clammy and the room spins.

"Help me get cleaned up. I'll be fine," I mumble. However, I'm actually starting to think that I will not be fine. But I'm too ill to care. This is all my fault, and it's what I get for trying to find love, I guess. I'm sure I deserve this. *Yes. I deserve whatever happens.* I've made lots of bad choices. *Sinner's choices*, the voice in my head tells me. *You are an unforgivable whore.* Yes. Yes. That seems right in my brain now garbled from blood loss.

Somehow, I get cleaned up again with a lot of assistance from Marie. After she sponges me down with washrags and soap, she helps me get dressed with some effort in a fresh pair of pj's. My head hangs limply forward as my tangled dark hair covers my face. My arms flop at my sides, like a scarecrow who has lost its straw stuffing. Once I regain strength after dressing, Marie helps me stand from the commode. I have to drape my arm around her neck and lean on her heavily to be able to stand at all. The room swirls around me. We slowly make our way to her bedroom. As I glance toward my room, there is so much blood on my bed and floor that it now looks like a war zone. I stumble as we get near and collapse onto her bed. Falling right on top of the covers, I pass out.

When I awaken, it is morning, and Marie isn't home. I'm still in her bed, and I'm weaker than I was last night. I try to get out of bed and cannot. Something is very wrong. Now I'm sure of it. I feel so hot. *Well, hello there, tiny little monkey on the bed. What are you doing jumping up and down?* Wait. What? I rub my unfocused eyes. My arms feel heavy. There are clouds of pretty colors floating, right above my bed. Wow. How cool. I feel peaceful and *so* tired. I am extremely exhausted, and it takes all my strength to pick up my arm to feel my face for fever. I'm burning up, so my own fingers on my cheek feel like icicles. A fever should be highly concerning to me, but I am ill to the point of becoming disconnected from reality. I'm vaguely aware that I'm in real medical trouble here, but my mind is too gauzy to care. I lay there, hallucinating. I'm not sure if I'm awake or asleep. My spirit is aware of things happening. My body is not.

I have bled through my pads again. *Don't care. Too tired. Have to lie here. I am deathly ill.* My brain is fuzzy, but they said to watch for the symptoms: heavy bleeding, huge clots, high fever. I need a doctor, but I'm sure not going to go to one. "Call the number on the pamphlet or go to the ER if you have any concerns," the clinic had said. Yeah. Right. Dad will not find out about this nor will his girlfriend or the church people. *It's my time to go, I guess. I'm sorry, God, for everything.* I lay here. I'm not scared. I'm not anything, except just barely here. I don't know how long I've been like this, hovering between the physical and the spiritual realms.

I don't think Marie is home yet, and I'd like to see her before I die if I could. My mind is in and out of this world. Between here and … somewhere else. I feel like I have been hallucinating for hours. I turn my head and see the Bible on Marie's desk. I blink. I blink again. Yes. The Bible. Huh. It seems like a good idea in my jumbled, cottony mind to read the Bible before I leave this earth. I reach up with a weak arm and hit at it with the back of my hand. I'm too weak to actually grab it and pick it up. It topples onto the bed with a soft thud, just to the left of my head, its pages falling open on their own. *Good.* Next, I have to try to read it. That requires more movement, and I'm running out of what little strength I have. I twist and flop my legs to the left. Ok, now for my top half. I try my best to throw my torso in the direction that I want it to go. I'm lying on my left side now, gazing at the Bible's open pages. I'm so hot. And so thirsty. And so tired. I nod off and then jolt awake.

Bible. Read the Bible. I reminisce back to my younger days in church. In the Midwest, everyone goes to church as much as possible. Three times a week is the bare minimum. I have gone to church like that my entire childhood and again, intermittently as a young adult. I'm sure I know every Bible story there is to know. I have read and studied this book many, many times. My mind drifts—Samson, Joseph, Esther, Moses, and of course, Jesus—my eyes close. *Read it.* I jerk awake. *What? Who said that? Read it. Read it. Oh, the Bible. Yes.* I slowly push myself up onto one elbow, supporting my floppy head with my hand. I lean down close to the pages because my eyes are so dry and my vision so blurry that I can hardly see. I weakly rub my eyes. Now, what verses has this Bible flopped open to? I expect to see a familiar story. A good Baptist always knows chapter and verse. I scan and read the page. I read the notation, Mark 5:24. I don't think I know this one. I start to read.

The story is about a woman who has been bleeding for years. She has been to every doctor and has spent all she has on treatments that have failed. She is considered unclean in her culture and is not to be around people because of her condition. She thinks to herself that if she can just touch the hem of Jesus's robe, she will be healed. So she presses into the crowd, bustling around Him, and stretches her arm forward to grab anything of His that she can reach. Grasping desperately through the mass of people thronging about Him, she just barely touches His robe. He instantly knows someone with faith in His healing power has touched Him. Jesus also knows that the person who just touched Him has been healed. Who was it? It was the unclean and bleeding woman. *She* has been healed. I read this all in perfect clarity. No fuzzy brain. I am not confused. I have never heard this Bible story before. Ever. *So Jesus healed a woman with the same kind of problem as me? Oh.* My soul seems to speak to itself deep down inside me. *"Then I will be ok. Good."* Peace comes over me as this sentiment falls into my spirit. I feel like Jesus is telling me I will be fine because He is healing me. I drop into an exhausted and feverish sleep.

I don't know how long I sleep, but Marie wakes me when she gets home. I feel awful. No matter how much I rest, it is not enough. Also, I'm still going to the bathroom very often to clean myself up because of the heavy bleeding. I am able to eat some now, and I am keeping down some fluids. My strength is slowly returning, so I require much less physical help getting up than I did a few days earlier. I ask Marie what day it is and am shocked to learn that ten days have passed since the abortion. I thought it was only a day or two. Time has escaped me.

My hallucinations have stopped. My fever has broken. The bleeding is slower than it was, and I guess it will continue for a while. I think of Mark 5:24 and the lady in the story. I say to myself and Marie, "If Jesus did it for her, He will do it for me. I am healed." Although I don't look healed, and I definitely don't deserve to be, I do believe this is true. I'm still having lots of problems, but I am getting just slightly better each day. I still feel as sick as a dog, but I'm no longer on death's door step. Somehow, I'm sure that I have been miraculously healed even though symptoms persist. Have I mentioned that I don't deserve anything from God, especially after what I did? He's healing me in spite of everything. That's grace and mercy. My heart feels content and my emotions settle after everything that has occurred. That is healing from God's hand too. There is simply no other explanation.

It's been four weeks since that horrendous day, and I still cannot function or do anything normally yet. The fatigue and bleeding are still constant, but I am growing stronger day by day. I can sit up for several hours at a time now. That's a big improvement. I can also walk a few feet, and I'm forcing myself to eat soups and crackers through the persistent nausea. I am definitely but slowly getting better. And I have not doubted that I will live and become totally well since the moment I read Mark 5:24.

In that moment, even though what I have done and been through isn't nice or pretty, and even though many, many times, I have sinned, God still loves me. That knowledge has started to heal my heart and soul as well as my body. I was looking for love in the wrong way. I just needed to be still, listen, and have a life-altering moment with God. I needed Him to touch my heart. In one second, everything was clear to me. As messed up as I was, and even with all the terrible things I've done, I *am* forgiven, loved, and healed. *This* is the love I have been searching for to fill the gaping hole inside me.

No man could ever love me like I needed to be loved until I let God love me, mend me, and restore me. This love from God does exist, and it is life-changing. It's not in a joint, a bottle of whiskey, or a one-night stand. It's not even in the front church pew with the deacon's wife. It's in an intimate moment with God. And it can happen anywhere. Anytime. Anywhere you are, He is. And so, there His most gracious love is also. Knowing His love will help you learn to love yourself, and that's when life begins to come full circle. It's only just begun for me.

Luca: A Few Years Later

LIFE IS GREAT, and every single day is going pretty dang good for once. I've got my own apartment and a nice job, and I even adopted a dog.

I woke up this morning, alive and healthy. I found a church I love, and I think I'm about to officially have a boyfriend. Since I found God (again) after my nightmarish abortion ordeal, my life has really turned around.

First, let me tell you about work. I got a job at a doctor's office as a receptionist. I didn't have experience, but they are a small practice and agreed to give me on-the-job training. The office is amazing. I am very grateful to have work I enjoy that also provides for all my needs. I moved out of Marie's and got my own place. I just needed to do that for me. We're still great friends. I just needed a whole new beginning again. Once I got all settled in my cozy two-bedroom apartment, I decided I needed a companion. So I went to the shelter and adopted a dog. He's a black German Shepherd, and the staff there said he's about four years old. I named him Goliath because he's huge. We take walks and play fetch and pal around everywhere together. He's a great guard dog, and he loves me. I've found more unconditional love in life with this dog than I did with most people. Goliath's my buddy.

At Happy Tails Shelter where I found him, I also found a great guy, and that's really what I want to tell you about. I'm so excited! Picture it: There I was, hands busy with my new, huge, black furball leashed up beside me, joyously out of control. Goliath was in an excited, slobbery, frenzy of newfound freedom. All 110 pounds of him. I, also, am 110 pounds, for the record. I'm sure we were a sight to behold.

Anyway, there we were in the parking lot. I was trying to get him to jump into my car so I could pack in the bowls, toys, and food that came with him. My arms were overloaded, and Goliath, who's leash was wrapped around my hand, was lunging and leaping all over, pulling my arms apart like I was a marionette. I was really struggling not to drop everything or let go of the leash. Goliath was rambunctious, overjoyed, and not listening to me at all. He was too excited to quit jumping around; plus, he was trying to chase anything that moved. Goliath would make eye contact with me when I'd tell him to get in the car, but then he would tuck his head playfully, front paws down, butt up in the air, tail wagging at full speed, and try to take off again. Sometimes he'd zip toward a squirrel in the side yard; other times, it seemed like he just wanted me to take off running on an adventure with him. I ended up clumsily dropping the dog supplies all over the ground by the trunk of my car so I could get him wrangled under control. Instead, somehow, the slip-on green nylon all-in-one leash–collar combo the pound provided me slipped from my wrist, and he bolted across the lot, right toward a guy—a really hot guy—who had just parked and was stepping out of his car. Goliath plowed into him at what appeared to be one hundred miles per hour, knocking the guy back and down into his car seat. Thankfully, his car door was still open, or he would have landed on the ground.

The guy started laughing at Goliath's playful attack and kept petting him while, at the same time, wrapping his arms around Goliath's body to keep him captured as I ran over with the leash. He smiled up at me, our eyes met, and my heart skipped a beat. Goliath sat right down, panting, pink tongue hanging out, and gazing up at me innocently. I slipped the leash back over Goliath's head and apologized profusely, of course. The man was very understanding. And he was gorgeous. Introducing himself as William, he said he was there to drop off some donations for the shelter. *How very kind of him*, I thought. He's cute *and* nice? Noted. We started talking, and the next thing I knew, he asked if I wanted to go to dinner later in the week. Ladies, when a guy like William asks you out, you say yes. He was tall, strong, bald, and tattooed. He had twinkling blue eyes and smelled like a very delicious man-scented candle. His smile and laugh were contagious. I couldn't stop smiling around him even though I was trying. I figured my huge cheesy grin was making me look like some kind of lunatic or desperate psychopath.

Regardless, like a gentleman, William walked Goliath and me back over to my old rust bucket of a car and helped me load up all the dog supplies. Of course, Goliath, being a showoff, jumped right into the car this time. *Good boy*. Apparently, he prefers the front seat over the back seat. Go figure. Anyhow, I just kept talking to William and talking and talking and talking and talking. It was like I couldn't shut up. He made me nervous in a good way, and I felt excited around him. I also sadly realized that we were standing in a parking lot and that I would actually have to get into my car and drive away from him at some point. Bummer. We exchanged numbers and set up a date to meet for dinner at a local pizza and beer place. *Yes!* I finally made myself stop talking long enough to actually get in my car. Goliath and I pulled away, and I stuck my arm out the window, waving like a crazy parade queen until William was out of sight. I discussed all my feelings with Goliath on the way home. He sat there, listening like a gentleman the entire ride, and I'm sure he understood every word.

Today is date day! The plan is to meet at A Crust Above at five for pizza, wings, and beer. It's a locally owned pizza joint, plus it has a dog friendly patio, so William insisted that I bring Goliath. This lucky dog! William and I have talked for the past couple of days (and nights) on the phone and have found out that we get along really well. In two days, we have probably talked for seven or eight hours. That's a lot more than I talk to anyone else. I like him even more now than I did when we first met. He says he really likes me too. (Yay, me!) Every time he calls, I feel all warm and fuzzy inside, and I've found out a lot about him just in these few short days. For example, he's a doctor, he's new to town, he's looking for a job, and he loves pizza. He says he's "interested in a relationship," and although he hasn't exactly specified the "with me" part, I'm pretty sure it's implied. I hope I'm right because I sure get hot and bothered thinking about him and our upcoming date tonight, but I digress. And now, it's time for a shower. A cold one.

The clock seems to be ticking so slowly as I count down the hours until our very first date. I've showered, shaved my legs, blow dried my hair, put on make-up, and changed my outfit four times. I go feed Goliath. Then I stroll back to the bathroom to style my hair, curling it up as big as I am able to, then spray it with half a can of Rave so it stays put. I look like I just sauntered out of a Glamour Shots studio. Perfect! I'm pretty sure this hairstyle could withstand a tornado. Anyhoo, I take Goliath out to the bathroom and glance at the clock. I have thirty more minutes to kill before it's time to meet up with Bill, so I grab a ball and play catch with my pup in the living room. The doorbell chimes, but I'm not expecting anyone. Goliath goes crazy barking and runs toward the door on guard, a low growl in his throat. Cautiously, I look through my peephole. It's William!

I pull Goliath back as best I can, holding onto his collar, telling him, "It's ok," and opening the door with the other hand. I'm struggling with the furry beast. "Hurry up and get in here," I say laughing. Once the door is shut firmly, I let go of Goliath who promptly starts nudging William, whose hands are full of a gorgeous flower bouquet. William smiles and says he couldn't wait any longer to see me. *Yesss*, I think. I try to remain calm as he hands me the array of white roses and baby's breath wrapped in green paper, the scent of them already filling the room. I show him to the living room, telling him to make himself at home as I run and grab a mason jar from under the sink to use as a vase. Filling the jar with water and trimming the stems, I arrange them carefully, then set the display on the table. I cannot remember the last time anyone gave me flowers. I thank William profusely, his kind and romantic act surprising and delighting me. I feel special.

With the flowers situated, I walk back toward him. As soon as I get within arm's length, he grabs me, pulling me into him, and starts kissing me. Wow! He's a wonderful kisser! I love the way his arms feel wrapped around me as he holds our bodies close. After at least a solid minute of kissing, he pulls back, stares deeply into my eyes, and says, "I'm hungry."

Oh. "I'm hungry too," I say. I'm not sure if either of us is talking about pizza. Disclaimer: I'm actually being celibate (like, for the first time ever) in this season of my life and have been for some time. Of course, William doesn't know that yet. So it seems to me like we need to leave. Immediately. To go get that pizza and an ice-cold beer or two to cool us both down. I clip Goliath's leash onto his collar. The three of us walk together out the front door and hop into William's car.

The car is a convertible, so Goliath's long pink tongue hanging out flaps around in the breeze the entire way, a trail of his fur blowing in the wind behind us. When we get to the pizza joint, I find out that William really is a lover of all pizza. He's not picky about the crust type, size, or toppings. I'm strictly a veggie girl. And while William is a lover of all things pizza, I find out that he is not a lover of vegetables. So we end up ordering a half pepperoni, half veggie and an order of wings with ranch on the side. The wings are crispy, saucy, and fried to perfection. The pizza is hot, cheesy, and delicious. We sit cozied up on the enclosed patio. We converse comfortably in a dimly lit corner booth made from wooden pallets stamped "San Marzano Product of Italy Peeled Tomatoes." It has green vinyl-padded cushions for seats, and we share the same bench so that we can snuggle between bites.

The table's red-and-white-checked cloth and one small candle, warmly flickering at us through red glass, add to the romantic yet casual atmosphere. William's relaxed and welcoming personality makes it so easy for me to sit and talk to him for hours. It's fall, so the sun is already setting. Clear, round patio lights are strung up and glowing overhead, so we can stay here long after the sun sets. We get refills of our Peroni more than once. It's served ice cold from the tap in frosty glasses. Goliath is being surprisingly well-mannered. I swear, he senses how important this night is to me. He just lounges around lazily on the patio, thumping his tail happily at anyone who walks by. Every once in a while, we toss him a cheesy bite of pizza that he immediately devours. I laugh and drink and flirt. I rub my foot on William's leg under the table. He rubs my leg back with his. We've been intermittently holding hands or one of us is placing a hand on the other's thigh as we talk. We are slowly getting to know the feel of each other. It's an amazing date. I haven't felt this relaxed and comfortable with a man in a long, long time, actually, probably ever if I'm being honest.

This is all new, but I feel an ease around him that has been missing my whole life. We've been on our date so long now that the restaurant is starting to close. The waiter comes over, politely reminding us of the time, and we decide to order dessert. There are homemade cannoli on the menu, and we order two. I've got to go to the bathroom, so I rush to get back outside, not wanting to waste a second of our time together. William goes to the bathroom next, and as I relax and wait, his phone rings. I can't help but see the screen when it lights. It's face-up on the table where he left it. A picture of a young lady about our age appears, and the contact information that pops up says "My Girl." I am suddenly nauseated and ready to go.

My heart pounds, and I swear I can hear my blood thundering in my ears. The phone is still ringing as William gets back to the table. He looks down at it and then up at me. He can tell I have seen the caller id and that I'm bothered by what it says. Now I feel nervous and edgy; the joy I had is squelched. He sits down, reaching across the table and gently grabs my hand. He looks at me with concerned eyes. "That's the girl I just broke up with. I just haven't deleted her number yet," he says.

I look at him. Doubtful. "Uh-huh. Sure, it is," is all I can think to say as my mind races, full of negative thoughts. "I think we should call it a night." I have had such a great time. My spirit feels crushed after just finding the hope I felt with him tonight. Now, I'm emotionally back to square one. I have no idea if he's telling me the truth or not. I don't know him *that* well, and I have no idea what he wants from me in the long term. I don't know if he has a secret girlfriend. I don't actually know anything except that we get along really well and that I am very into him. I need to get out of here quickly. I feel like crying, and that's crazy because this is our first date!

William tells me he understands my sudden urgency to leave and politely pays the tab, getting the cannoli to go. We walk awkwardly and silently to the car. Even Goliath seems to feel the tension. He doesn't make a peep and hops right into the back of the convertible. Laying down, he lets out a huge, dramatic sigh as he rests his furry head on his front paws. On the short ride back to my place, William reassures me that he broke up with the girl who called the day after we met. He says he knew then that he wanted to be with me. He says he was going to ask me to be his girlfriend tonight. That all sounds very nice. And convenient. That would have been fabulous had she not called. It would be better if I never knew she existed, assuming he's telling me the truth. I have been screwed over so much in the past, I can't help but wonder if this is the truth or just another man who is busted lying and is now trying to keep the peace on all sides.

William insists on calling her in front of me to prove that they are broken up. My heart does a little hiccup. Who would do that unless they were telling the truth? "Ok," I say nonchalantly with a little shrug. I'm hoping to throw him off guard by agreeing to it. *Do it.* Distrust stirs in me, but so does hope. We sit in his car, now parked in front of my house as he dials her on speakerphone. It only rings once before she excitedly answers. My stomach is in knots. I'm hoping this call will prove something to me. Something good. William asks why she called him, and she starts rambling on about how she loves him and misses him. He politely interrupts after a minute or so and tells her that they are broken up for good and that she should stop calling him. She starts to whine, her voice rising about an octave. She needs him, she says, and they need to be together. She is nearly begging and sounds like she's going to cry. Cutting her off more firmly this time, he tells her that they are done and that he has a new girlfriend.

What?, I think. *Does he mean me?* He turns to face me and winks. A crooked grin appears, and one of his dimples starts to show as the smile grows larger. The nameless "My Girl" gets louder and starts shrieking obscenities at him. He just speaks loudly and sternly above her wailing. "Don't call me anymore!" He clicks the phone off and deletes her contact information. Shrugging, he looks at me with a twinkle in his eye. "Well, will you?"

"Will I what?" I ask.

"Will you be my girlfriend? Officially." My heart soars.

My face heats up and my ears turn red. "Yes!" I answer too excitedly. "Are there any other things"—I cough and start to nervous fidget—"that you need to tell me? Because now's the time …" I let my comment trail off.

"Nope. We're all good. I'm an open book," he responds. Opening the box of cannoli, he holds one up. "A peace offering." He holds it up to my mouth so I can have the first bite. Goliath suddenly flies up from the back seat and gulps the entire thing down in one swallow. We crack up. He's too cute to be upset. We split the other cannoli, guarding it with our lives from the fur ball. When we finish eating dessert in the car, William opens my car door and walks me to the front door. He gives me a respectable, gentle kiss on the lips, pets Goliath, and tells me he's really glad I'm his girlfriend. I can't stop grinning. I go to bed immediately after he drops me off since it's late. I fall asleep dreaming about good things for once.

And that's how we became a couple: over pizza, Peroni, and a phone call from a psycho ex. It's a beautiful beginning.

Eighteen Months Later

WILLIAM HAS STARTED his own practice, and I am now his front desk associate. I absolutely love it! We work together and play together every single day. We attend First Community Church and volunteer at their food bank, helping people in need in our community together too. We make a wonderful team, in my opinion. We do absolutely everything together. It's pretty cool when we can share working together *and* being in love. This experience is rare and special to find. We both say that our life together is a gift from God.

I am hoping that Wiliam proposes to me soon. (I mean, what girl doesn't hope that after a couple of years?) We are best friends and are madly in love. This relationship is amazing. Every day we get to spend together is awesome and a huge blessing to me. We each still live in our own places, but he is begging me to move in with him. I fall asleep at his house all the time anyway, and Goliath stays wherever I go.

I just want to do things in the healthiest way possible in this relationship. I want to at least be engaged with a wedding date planned before I move in. I feel safer that way since my life has been one big crash course in what can go wrong in dreams and relationships. I'm sure it's also some old PTSD coming up, but I can't help it. In this relationship, I also want to make sure I am honoring God, and that includes my choices about what I do in private. Our two-year anniversary is coming up very soon. I'm getting more excited and nervous about it every day because I'm hoping that's when he's going to ask me to marry him. Fingers crossed.

William and Luca: Two Year Anniversary

WILLIAM CALLS ME and says he's running late to the office. I'm already there, and I tell the patient waiting that we're running a few minutes past her scheduled appointment time. I'm catching up on emails and returning phone calls when William, known to the staff as "Doc," comes bursting through the back door carrying a huge vase of white roses (my favorite), a fresh latte, and singing, "Happy two-year anniversaaaryyy,", at the top of his lungs. He is all smiles and silliness and love. I can't help but grin, deeply moved by his thoughtfulness. *He is always so generous and romantic,* I think. I still get butterflies every time he's around.

Getting up from my office chair, I grab the huge vase from him, setting it on my desk. I take a slurp of the coffee as I tell him thank you, that I love him, and that he has a patient waiting. I give him a quick peck on the lips. Then I get back to the day's business but not before I pat his butt when he turns to walk to his office. He has a really cute butt. What can I say? My heart feels light. He's the best.

We see our patients throughout the day, and then I surprise him with my gift. I have blocked off his calendar for the afternoon and let the office staff go home early, which I *never* do. I have scheduled a massage for him at a nearby spa. I hand him an anniversary card with the information written inside. We are in the back office, and since we are out of sight of any patients that could accidentally straggle in, he quickly grabs my hips with both hands. Pulling me firmly toward him, he gives me a very passionate kiss now that the office is closed for the day. He lets go of my hips and pushes me gently but assertively against the wall. Protecting the back of my head with one of his hands, he then grabs my hair in his fist pulling it slowly and firmly, *just* hard enough to be a turn on, as he continues hungrily kissing me. Pressing his body against mine, his hands quickly move from one part of me to another. Gently exploring more than one sensitive area, I am starting to *really* like this. I reposition myself ever so slightly against him as he continues caressing me. It's getting spicy in here, and he has a massage to get to. I force myself to stop kissing him and pull away but not because I want to. "You get out of here now," I say breathlessly, "before you're late."

He pulls away, winking at me. "You got it, boss."

We'll go to dinner at our favorite wine bar later to celebrate and finish this make-out session afterward. I close up at the office and get home to take Goliath on a walk. Getting ready for our date I take my time and use extra care. I'm not a fan of dressing up or of anything fancy, but I want to look extra nice tonight. Just in case there's a proposal. A girl definitely wants to look her best for that.

William meets me over at my place after his massage. He ran home to quickly shower and change. He has on the expensive cologne he rarely wears that I love, and he smells delicious. I'm as dressed up as I've ever been in my life, and I'm excited for our date at Vino, our favorite wine bar. William looks relaxed and handsome as ever. Hugging me, he lets me know he's just had the best massage of his life. I breathe in a big sniff of his seductive, smokey aroma. My mouth waters just a bit, and I warm with a flush of arousal. Taking a step back to admire my dress, William slowly moves his eyes up and down my body, telling me I look "ravishing." I will definitely take that compliment! I blush, a bit embarrassed, but I'm glad I took extra time getting ready. Since we're both starving, we head out.

Arriving at Vino, we are shown to our reserved table in an elegant, dimly lit private dining room. A bottle of our favorite bubbly is chilled and waiting in a silver stand by our velvet seats. As a romantic touch, a crystal vase full of red roses adorns the clothed table. Since our first date, whenever possible, William and I always enjoy sitting on the same side of the table close to each other so we can snuggle a bit during meals. And that's exactly what we do tonight as we are seated. I feel grateful and hopeful and very in love, sitting here beside him.

Ordering our favorite meal, which is a huge charcuterie board overflowing with fruits, olives, meats, pickles, cheeses, and breads, we sip on our champagne and enjoy each other's company. When the board comes out, we eat, take turns laughing and feeding each other grapes and olives, and talk about our future. William asks me to move in with him (again). I tell him (again) that I need to be sure our relationship is a full, long-term commitment, not just some shacking-up deal. I've already been there, done that, and he knows it burned me. I need something tangible. Proof to the world that we are each other's one and done. That we are both fully committed to forever.

This is my way of hinting at a proposal, and it's definitely not the first time I've said something similar. He stares at me with his sparkling blue eyes and gently says he understands. He tells me again how much he loves me. Now I'm starting to get nervous. If he *is* going to propose, this would be the perfect time since the conversation is leaning that way. I'm anxious but also excited. My palms start to sweat. I wonder if he can read my thoughts. I'm actually thinking on repeat, *Ask me, I'll say yes. Ask me, I'll say yes.* My heart is pounding while I'm trying to remain casual. I'm starting to fidget. I can't help it. I clear my throat three times. There's a pause in the conversation, and I think, *This is it*! If he's going to ask, it will be right now! I hold my breath. I tell myself to relax. He loves me. Of course he does. But my mom's voice tumbles through my mind. *You are unlovable, Luca*! *Just shut up*, I think as I wait. It is unbelievable that her words still have this much effect on me. I haven't seen her in years. I shrug these thoughts off as William says we can discuss our living situation more, later at home, and changes the subject. That's it. Nothing. Nada. No proposal.

I feel deflated. I try to hide my disappointment. I really thought tonight would be the night. I start to wonder if he thinks I'm just not quite good enough. You know, not exactly wife material. With a past like mine, I've got to wonder. These dang bad thoughts always creep in. Self-doubt is wild. I try to stop it, but it's really hard.

They say actions speak louder than words. His actions or lack thereof are feeding all my doubts. Big time. We finish our delicious meal, and I'm ready to go. My heart is slightly wounded, and I'm telling myself it will all be ok. I'm trying not to be a crybaby about this. *Be mature*, I tell myself in my head. I am so thankful to have William. I just want more. More of him that is. Not more stuff. I want him to tell the world that I'm his. Legally and forever. I want his name. I want to be his family. Maybe guys in general just don't understand that part of a woman's psyche.

Anyway, it was a beautiful date and dinner, and I am very thankful for what we have. I count my blessings as he offers a romantic toast to us with our final glasses of bubbles. We decide to skip dessert for snuggling at my house on the couch. I'm ready to change out of this fancy outfit and into something more comfortable. He says he's ready to watch the last part of the Chiefs game if we get home in time. We politely flag down the waiter and pay the check along with a generous tip (of course) and head out.

Once at my place, we pull into the driveway and park. Walking to my porch, we decide the game plan will be for me to take Goliath out to do his business while William showers. Holding hands as we walk through the door, Goliath comes running at us full speed. Bursting through our arms and breaking them apart, he is his usual spastic self. This reminds me of playing Red Rover as a kid. Laughing, we pat him on the head and tell him he's a good boy. I rustle around in the closet to find his leash and my flip flops. Finding the leash, I clip it onto his collar, kick my fancy shoes off, and slip on my flip- flops. I give William a quick kiss as he heads up to the shower. Goliath and I wander the neighborhood until we are both panting and thirsty. We've walked at least a couple of miles.

By the time we get back, the sun is down, and I've thrown my hair up into a sweaty ponytail. Walking into the house, I don't see William anywhere. I stop and listen for a second because I figure he's already in the living room, flopped on the couch watching the game. I don't hear a sound. "Hello…" I say loudly, my voice echoing in the silence. Taking Goliath's leash off and tossing it back into the closet, I quickly glance around the main level, then hop up the steps two at a time toward the bedrooms. "You in here?" I ask, poking my head into an empty bathroom. The shower is wet, and his damp towel is in the laundry basket, so I know he's got to be here somewhere. Still, anxiety creeps in. *Where is he*?

Goliath is whining at the rear patio door, so I head back down. My apartment isn't very big, so by the time I get downstairs, I have already looked in every room and know that William isn't inside. Something seems a little off. I'm suddenly edgy. Goliath runs to me, nudging my hand, then runs to the back door, nudging the knob, then runs back to me. *Ok.* I take the hint and open the door to the small, enclosed backyard.

I can't see outside because now it's dark, and the red-and-white-checkered shade on the kitchen window is pulled down. Trusting that the darkness is safe since Goliath isn't growling and is actually straining to go out, I pull the door open. He darts into the yard. Suddenly, music is playing, a romantic country tune by Randy Travis called "Forever and Ever, Amen." I've always loved it, but where is it coming from? My eyes start adjusting to the darkness, and as they do, a flicker of light appears to my left. A now glowing candle illuminates the small wrought-iron table and two chairs I have on the patio. William stands beside the table, handsome as ever. "Hello gorgeous," he says. "Come over here and sit down. It's time for dessert." I'm shocked to see him but relieved that he's out here. *But what is he up to?*

Music continues to play softly as I step toward the table. William pulls out a chair for me, and as I sit down, I now see that there's an opened bottle of red wine and what appears to be a souffle (my favorite dessert of all time) on the small table that he has set. My heart swells with love at this romantic gesture. I'm completely caught off guard. "Thank you, honey. I was worried when I couldn't find you inside. What is all of this? It's very sweet."

"I love you and I want you to know how special you are to me," he says. He pours wine into our glasses and gazes at me lovingly.

"Are you going to sit down?" I ask since he is still standing by my chair. The souffle looks delicious, and a dessert like that can't just wait forever. He looks at me, his expression serious.

The next thing I know, he is down on one knee, pulling a black velvet box out of his pocket. Before all of this can register, he has flipped open the lid, a beautiful diamond ring now glinting in the candlelight. "Do me the honor of being my wife, Luca," he says softly. "Will you marry me?" There he kneels, freshly showered, looking and smelling delicious. Here I am, shocked, sweaty, and covered in dog hair from the walk. My mind is screaming *yes*! William fidgets beside me and emits a small cough, clearing his throat. I then realize I have not said anything out loud.

Looking into his eyes, he seems steady but nervous. A sweat has broken out across his brow. "Oh! Yes! Yes! Yes," I scream. "Of course I'll marry you!" I grab him and kiss him right where he kneels. We can hardly stop kissing, smiling, and laughing. I am not a crier, but this once-in-a-lifetime romantic moment has me tearing up.

"Give me your hand," he says reverently. I hold it out, but it's trembling from excitement as he starts to slip the most beautiful antique band I have ever seen onto my ring finger. "It was my grandmother's." The ring is white gold with a fairly large round center diamond with smaller diamonds on each side. It fits perfectly and glimmers in the candlelight.

"I love it, and I love you. Thank you, William,", I reply. Goliath gives an excited yap as he eyeballs the souffle. I laugh. "Oh no, you don't, boy! You aren't getting dessert this time." He barks again, wagging his tail as William gets up from where he has been kneeling. Setting the empty ring box on the table and slowly walking back around to me with a smoldering hot gaze, he wraps his strong arms around my body, picking me right up off my chair. William's mouth presses passionately against mine. Our once calm breaths have turned into short gasps of delight as our bodies become entangled and our kisses more intense. After several minutes of this heated backyard exchange, we pull ourselves away from each other to catch our breath. I lick my wet lips as William reluctantly backs away while keeping his eyes locked with mine.

He finds his chair and sits down. Staring at me with a sparkle in his eye and picking up his wineglass, he says, "To us, our future, and our family." He glances at the fluffy dessert. "Let's eat this thing so we can go upstairs!"

We clink our glasses and drink to us. The souffle practically melts in our mouths. The warm, gooey center can only be described as sexual. We savor every single bite. Then William swoops me up into his strong arms, carrying me right up the backyard steps and into the bedroom where we burn off some of those French pastry calories after which we fall blissfully to sleep wrapped in my thick, down comforter and each other's arms.

William and Luca: One Year Later

THE MEDICAL PRACTICE is thriving, and we have ads all over town to hire more staff. Since the engagement, I moved into William's place. We've been living together for the past twelve months. It is absolutely heaven on earth. Life with him is more than I ever imagined in my wildest dreams and prayers. I was so excited and happy when he proposed that I even called Dad and told him about our engagement. I thought he'd be excited. Sadly, but not surprisingly, he's still drunk with Jan all the time and didn't really care. I won't be talking with them again anytime soon. Now that I've got some stability in life, I've learned to start creating healthy boundaries for my new family. I'm really proud of myself for that! The support of William has made me realize how much crap I have put up with from other people for no reason. I am officially starting to grow a healthy backbone and learning to be assertive, not aggressive like I used to be.

While William and I were in the middle of wedding planning, a slight hiccup occurred. Several months ago, we found out that I'm pregnant! William is thrilled! We both are. We've discussed it and decided that instead of spending a lot of money on a big wedding, we would rather elope and save the cash for our growing family. We're comparison shopping for cute, affordable weekend destinations now. I'm not picky. All I care about is that we're together. Well, that and that we get to eat wedding cake. White cake with buttercream frosting. I mean, come on. My wedding does *have* to have a cake. I'm not a monster!

Currently, I'm almost six months pregnant and really starting to show. My pregnancy is definitely obvious. I'm feeling pretty good, and I'm still working full time. I manage the office staff at the business, and I am still looking for another front office person, another nurse, and a groundskeeping-cleaning person. Work is swamped, which is great. The sooner we can hire more people, the better. Then the practice can take on more patients. And more patients equals more money. It's a very exciting time for us. William and I don't have the hours in the day or the energy to keep cleaning the office and the bathrooms, mowing the grass, picking up trash in the parking lot, doing all the administrative stuff needed to run the business, plus continuing to do everything at home and get ready for the baby. I've got help-wanted ads posted everywhere.

The office schedule is packed again today. We count it as a blessing that we have back-to-back patients with no time for any of us to take a lunch break. We've got several new patients and the second nurse we hired is doing great, but we still need a third. The two front desk associates barely have time to breathe between calls and check-ins, but they are superstar employees. William has been tirelessly seeing patients all day. I'm manning one of the phones in the back office, trying to catch up on calling patients back about their lab work and scheduled tests. The front desk girls are checking people in, rooming them, collecting payments, cleaning between patients, answering calls, and doing scheduling. It's crazy. But good crazy.

William suddenly pops out of a patient room, washes his hands, and pulls a sandwich from the small fridge we have, eating it as he stands. He looks over the next patient's chart. Another physician is on hold for him. He tells me he's got to go to the bathroom before he takes the call as he quickly swallows the bite he has in his mouth and wraps the rest of the sandwich back up. He makes a beeline to the restroom as Brian, one of our front desk associates, walks by and tells me a job applicant is out front. I'm really too busy to talk to anyone else, but I tell Brian I will be there as soon as I can to meet with the tentative employee since we are desperate for help.

I pull Sarah, the other front desk associate, back to my desk to continue calling patients about their test results while I go to the front.

Our nurse, Lisa, steps out of an exam room and lets Doc know as he comes out of the restroom that his next patient is ready. He nods to her and says "thanks," first picking up the phone that has a call waiting on it as he takes a swig of coffee. I hurry toward the waiting area to speak with the applicant.

As I walk past Brian, he quickly shoves the filled-out resumé and application at me. I'm in a rush and don't even glance down. I grab the stack of papers and head through the door that separates the back-office area and the lobby. I look over at Brian, tilting my head to the waiting area. "I'll be out there if anyone needs me." I'm already through the door when he tells me the guy's name is Jack.

As his sentence registers in my brain and the door clicks shut behind me, I look up. And there he is. My ex. The jerk. The vile narcissist. The man who almost killed me and did force me to kill our baby. Jack. I am stunned. Here in *my* waiting room full of *our* patients is the man from hell. He looks at his application in my hand and looks back up at my face.

The millisecond recognition of me clicks in his eyes. I am no longer a poor, helpless teen. I have changed for the better over the years and am now a beautiful, accomplished woman. I cannot say the same about him. His life has gone drastically downhill over the years. He steps toward me, closing the space between us, and smiles. I freeze, feeling like all the air is being sucked out of the room. I feel trapped. In the full waiting room, everyone else disappears as my mind sharply focuses on and assesses Jack. My face remains stoic although every muscle in my body tenses as I change my stance ever so slightly. My fight-or-flight reflex is in full force. My body remembers everything. The last time I saw him, he was threatening to kill me. He forced me to do the unthinkable. Now, here he is. Acting casual. Again. My mind reels. My heart slams in my chest, and sweat trickles down my spine. *No*, I tell myself. *I will* not *let him intimidate me.*

I am nauseated and silently freaking out. I force myself to make direct eye contact.

Speak, I tell myself. I need to remain in control and appear strong. "Is this your application?" I question him.

"Hey. Yeah. It's been a long time. How are ya, sugar? What are you doing here?" he responds.

'Sugar?' Are you kidding me? He has the audacity to use his old pet-name for me? I think. He's acting all nonchalant and friendly, just like the disgusting narcissist that he is. He has absolutely no regard for what he put me through. None. Now, I'm not scared, I'm just pissed. Out of habit, I guess, I say a quick, silent prayer for strength and courage and calmness. Calm does overtake me. My near panic is gone immediately. In its place is boldness.

I feel fierce. I quickly look around the room, full of patients. This is *my* life. This is the life William and I have built together. *Our* patients. *Our* waiting room. *Our* building. *Our* dream. And Jack needs to go. I straighten my shoulders and hold my head high. Looking directly at him and speaking assertively and professionally, I tell him that my fiancé and I own this business. I tell him that we have no position for him, nor will we ever. I calmly walk over to the trash can, step on the pedal that opens the lid, and drop his application straight down into it, never averting my eyes from him. He glances around the room at the people waiting who are now watching him. He pauses briefly, deciding what to say in response to me. He starts telling me about his life now. That he has hit hard times, is getting divorced, and really needs this job. I cut him off. I have boundaries. And I don't care. He then starts to compliment me. He tries to go on and on about how good I look and how he has wondered about me. He motions with his head toward my rounded stomach and says, "I see you're pregnant—"

I interrupt him for the second time. "You need to leave now and never come back here. Ever." As I'm speaking, the office door quietly opens behind me, and just like that, William steps beside me, putting his arm around me.

"Everything ok here?" He looks at me. Of course he has heard the story *of* Jack, but he has never *seen* Jack. And he has no idea it's him standing right here, right now. That's a *very* good thing for Jack's sake.

I look up at William. "It is now. This guy was just leaving." Without another word, Jack turns and shuffles dejectedly out of the office. I smile up at my sweet William. I swear, he and I are connected. He never comes out to the waiting room, yet here he stands. My protector. My love with perfect timing. I place my hand gently on my growing belly, feeling overwhelmingly blessed with all that God has given me, regardless of my mistakes. God's mercy, forgiveness, and grace really are wonderful. I don't deserve them, but He gives them to me freely anyway. "Mrs. Jones, we are ready for you. Come on back." I open the door and smile.

I know I am loved by God, by William, and soon, I will be loved by our little baby too. I am Luca. Regardless of my past, I know now that I am lovable. In fact, I always was.

Resources for Help

SAMHSA (Substance Abuse and Mental Health Services Administration) Hotline: 1-800-662-HELP

Alcoholics Anonymous: 1-212-870-3400

National Drug Helpline: 1-844-289-0879

Al-Anon (support for family members of alcoholics): 1-888-4AL-ANON

National Domestic Violence Hotline: 1-800-799-7233

Option Line (Pregnancy): 1-800-712-4357

National Maternal Mental Health Hotline (pregnant or just had a baby) – text anytime to talk with a counselor: 1-833-TLC-MAMA

National Parent Hotline (Parents Anonymous): 1-855-427-2736

Veterans Crisis Hotline: Dial 988, then press 1 or text 838255

Jesus Loves You!

About the Author

A Missouri native, Amy Dennis is a nurse with more than twenty-five years of experience. She met her amazing husband, Bill, while they worked together in the emergency room of a major trauma center. She is also the mom of two wonderful grown sons, two daughters-in-love, and two grandchildren. At church, she has enjoyed serving on worship teams, working as a greeter, and serving in children's ministry. Amy feels God has called her to be an encourager of those who have not had it easy in life.

In her spare time, Amy and her husband enjoy listening to live music, visiting breweries, traveling to be with family, and vacationing in the mountains or at the beach. Sometimes on cold, rainy days, Amy just hunkers down in bed reading—because cleaning can wait. She and her husband, along with their cat and dog, currently reside in Tennessee.

This is her third book, and her first novella.

www.ingramcontent.com/pod-product-compliance
Lightning Source LLC
LaVergne TN
LVHW090519110826
845146LV00003B/919

* 9 7 9 8 9 8 9 1 6 4 6 2 2 *